PRAISE FOR JESUS AND JOHN

"Adam McOmber's *Jesus and John* is an unsettling and sumptuously written reimagining of the gospels that blends religious and sensual ecstasy in a haunting and incantatory brew. Riveting and unmissable."

Robert Levy, author of *The Glittering World* and *Anaïs Nin at the Grand Guignol*

"There are many occult horror novels out there, but *Jesus and John*'s fully articulated gnostic horror puts it in a class all its own—as if Lovecraft had rewritten the Nag Hammadi codices. Beautifully written, heretical, and profoundly humane, this is a book about destabilizing one's entire sense of reality and revealing the unreal lurking within."

Brian Evenson, author of *Song for the Unraveling of the World*

"In Adam McOmber's lucid dream of a novel, the beloved disciple follows the risen Yeshua on a voyage across the sea to the eternal city. Within the streets of Rome, they will come to the door of a mysterious structure known as the Gray Palace, within whose walls wait horrors and revelations. A contemporary descendant of such works as Par Lagerkvist's *Barabbas* and Nikos Kazantzakis's *Last Temptation of Christ*, *Jesus and John* looks at the greatest story ever told through fresh, kaleidoscopic lenses and discovers marvels."

John Langan, author of *Children of the Fang and Other Genealogies*

"*Jesus and John* turns a fresh, fantastical eye to the familiar story of Jesus and the apostles and other religious tales."

Foreword Reviews

JESUS AND JOHN

ADAM McOMBER

Published by LETHE PRESS
lethepressbooks.com

ISBN: 9781590216736

Library of Congress Cataloging-in-Publication Data
available on request

Cover Design by MATTHEW REVERT
Interior design by INKSPIRAL DESIGN

For Brad

The Word was made flesh. And the Word dwelt among us.

This, according to Peter's book.

But I, called John and only John, know a truer story still. For I remember how His flesh felt against mine. The groove of the breastbone, the sinew of the arm. As if His body had been fashioned to answer some prayer I'd been repeating ever since I was a boy. Had my own father discovered my longings, he would have drowned me in the sea. Yet this stranger had come, kind and gentle, the remnants of some finer world still clinging to His limbs. And though He gathered me along with all the rest, I was to become, for Him, something more.

I remember now the taste of Him: chalk from the cliffs of Arbel and smoke from the village fires. We slept in a room apart from the others. The air was hot, long after the sun had set. We lay upon our pallet and listened to the wind move the cypress trees in the garden beyond. He was long-armed, thin. He touched me in the darkness, fingers cool upon my breast.

He said, "John, I will tell you things I cannot tell the others."

And, I confess, I did not understand His meaning then. I did not know that words could open like a mouth, and a listener could be swallowed.

I was young, a downy beard upon my cheeks and all my strength about me. And I was glad that He had chosen me, glad He had taken me from the boats and the sea and the tangled fishermen's nets.

I kissed His neck, His lips. I looked into His eyes, so dark they appeared almost painted, and I said, "Tell me what you must, my Lord, my Yeshua. Tell me and I promise I will always listen."

†

HE DID NOT speak His secrets then, nor did He speak them in the days that followed. It was not until the third day after His death that the revelations began. For on that day Mary, called Magdala, came to us with news.

I was in the room above the temple with Peter born as Simon. The others had gone off into the streets. Some of them had wept and torn their clothes. Others had grown still and silent, as if they themselves had died and were now buried beneath a stone.

Peter and I had known each other since we were boys, yet I cannot say we'd ever called each other friend. Dark-haired and forceful, he spoke with a Zealot's conviction. As a youth, he'd lived for a time with the warlike men in the caves at Qumran. And it was those men who'd first called him Peter, meaning "rock." Even in my earliest memories, Peter is there commanding us, dressed in his tattered brown tunic, a length of fisherman's rope tied about his waist. He behaved as if he was some noble warrior or great man of the temple. At night, he would gather us around a fire on the pebbled shores of Galilee. And there, he'd tell us stories, speaking as if he imagined we were a crowd of thousands.

I remember one such tale about a fabulous city sunk beneath the sea. Peter said the city lay just under the weathered hulls of our fathers' fishing boats, all golden towers and jewel-encrusted domes. And though the city was finer than Sidon or even Babylon, it had been forgotten. "But we sons of Galilee must remember," Peter said. "We are the descendants of that great city. And when our fathers call upon us to pull the lead rope or mend our nets with a meager piece bone, we must imagine those grand streets and shining courts. They will not be lost forever beneath the waves."

After Yeshua's death, Peter no longer told such stories. Instead, he sat in the room above the temple, grimly sharpening his sword. Unlike Peter, I sharpened no blade after Calvary. I sat at the window of the upper room and looked down at the market square below. I did not see the baskets of dried fish and vessels of date wine. Instead, I pictured the sea, the stony beaches there and leagues of men. I thought of my own father and my poor half-mad mother, and I wished, somehow, I could return to them, to be a boy again at their feet. Had Peter heard me speak such a desire, he would have ridiculed me, told me I was not a man. But I did not care what Peter thought. My dreams, I believed, were my own.

That evening, Mary called Magdala entered the upper room as the setting sun turned bronze on the horizon. She was dressed in mourning robes, and though the room was full of lamps, she chose to stand in shadow. Mary removed her veil and held it in her hands. Her eyes were wide. Her mouth, oddly slack. And though I wanted nothing more than to remain alone in my own silent mourning, I forced myself to speak. "What is it, Mary? What's wrong?"

She stared at me in silence, a fact that caused even greater concern. For Mary was neither meek nor circumspect. Her husband, a wealthy merchant from the East, had forbidden her to follow us. Yet like so many in our loyal band, Mary refused to listen. On more than one occasion, she'd sold fine bracelets from her ankles and wrists to ensure we had food to eat. Often, she sat with the men in the shade of the date palms, asking questions and offering prayers.

I wondered if a soldier had brought harm to her. Peter had told me that three Roman soldiers fell upon Bartholomew on his way to the bathing pool. And another had drunkenly thrown stones at Thomas as he walked on a road near the palace.

"Did someone frighten you?" I asked. "Did they try to hurt you?"

Peter looked up from his sword, dark brow furrowed. "If there's news, tell it plainly, Magdalene. And if there isn't, then leave us."

Mary turned slowly toward Peter. She made no sound and, for a moment, did not even appear to breathe.

"Are you unwell?" I said, standing from my seat at the window, intending to go to her.

"The tomb," Mary said finally. And her words sounded strange, as if they were not words at all.

"What about the tomb?" I said.

"I was there with the other women," she said. "We prayed. All of us. Then, the others departed. They went to prepare food. But I stayed. I wanted to say more prayers."

"You've always been good about saying your prayers," I said.

"I knelt on the ground before the stone that covers the mouth of the tomb. Do you know the stone, John?"

"I do."

"And have you put your hands upon it?" she asked.

"I have."

"Then you know it is a heavy stone."

I glanced at Peter who appeared to have forgotten his sword. "A heavy stone indeed," I said.

Mary twisted the black veil between her fingers. "The

hour grew late. I worried about robbers. It was Thomas who told me about robbers in the graveyard."

"Thomas likes to tell his stories," I said. "But he means no harm."

Mary closed her eyes. "I knelt on the ground, very near the stone. I believed that, if I was close enough, He would protect me from the robbers, just as He has always protected us. Didn't He protect us, John?"

"He did," I said. "He always did."

"I nearly put my face upon the rock. And that's when I heard..." Mary faltered.

"What did you hear?"

"Speak plainly," Peter said. "Don't draw the story out in a womanish way."

"A scratching," Mary said, "at the edges of the stone. Something trapped inside the tomb."

"Trapped?" Peter leaned forward.

"Clawing," Mary said. "A terrible noise. All around the edges."

"Well, what was it?" Peter said. "Some animal?"

She dragged her fingers through her hair. "Not an animal. That's what I've come to tell you. I don't think it was an animal at all."

†

PETER AND I ran to the tomb yard at the outskirts of the city. The many graves stood like small white ships, and the sky above was a darkening sea. Together, we rolled back the stone that covered the entrance to the tomb. For though the rock was heavy, two men could move it if they used their strength. The burial chamber was a narrow, dim cave. And I saw immediately that the shelf where we'd laid Him was empty.

"Desecrators," Peter said through gritted teeth. "I knew they'd come. The soldiers must have told them where we buried Him."

"But why would they roll stone back into place?" I said. "Why not leave the tomb open for everyone to see?"

"They'll drag the body into some field," Peter said. "Birds will pick His flesh. We have to—" He hesitated then, gazing into one dark corner of the tomb, fingers curled around the hilt of his sword.

I peered into the shadows too and saw, standing there, a tall gaunt figure draped in the length of a burial shroud. Funeral oils stained the shroud. And the boney form swayed from side to side, as a blade of tall grass might sway in a gentle wind.

"What is that, John?" Peter asked.

I didn't reply, though I knew the answer well enough. I recognized the man who stood there in the corner of the tomb, even though His features were hidden.

"John," Peter said again. "Who stands there in the shadows?"

The figure shifted, twitching its hands.

"Yeshua," I said softly.

Peter made a low sound at the back of his throat, the

growl of a frightened animal. "How do you know it's Him?"

"The way He stands," I said. "The way He moves." But, in truth, I simply knew Him. I'd lain with Him, touched His contours in the dark.

"Tell Him to lie down again," Peter said flatly.

"What?"

"He'll listen to you, John. He's always listened to you."

I turned to the figure. "Yeshua? Is it really you standing there?"

"Tell Him now," Peter said. "He must not stand if He is dead."

"Yeshua..."

The figure shuffled its feet, ambling forth. Perhaps it moved toward the sound of my voice or perhaps it merely sensed the fading light at the mouth of the cave.

Peter drew his sword but did not raise it.

The shroud fell away, revealing a naked body beneath. The bearded face I knew so well looked etched. Both eyes were closed, sealed with wax. The jaw hung low, exposing teeth and a long dark tongue. His flesh glowed faintly in the light, as the women had dusted it with myrrh, and His member hung limp and useless between His legs.

I looked at Peter, hoping that he might provide some further command. Yet he only stared dumbly as the body approached.

"Yeshua," I called. "Please stop. I know you don't mean to frighten us."

But Yeshua did not stop. He continued to move toward the mouth of the cave, shuffling His feet as He came.

†

PETER AND I ran like frightened children. We hurried back to the city, to the room above the temple. Once there, we barred the door with heavy furnishings. The room itself was empty. Mary called Magdala had gone to be with the women. The others had not yet returned. Peter covered his face and knelt in a corner. At first, I thought he prayed. But when he raised his head to look at me, there was terror on his face. "It was some wraith," he said. "Or worse than that." I'd never seen Peter in such a state, not even when we'd learned the guards had taken Yeshua away. Peter had believed we would find robbers at the tomb or even Roman soldiers. Someone to fight. But instead we'd encountered something that he could not challenge, a figure he could not even comprehend.

I thought about the face in the cave. Yeshua's face. Our own Yeshua. He'd looked sick, possibly starved. "Perhaps we should not have run," I said.

Peter stared at me as if I'd gone mad. "Have you not heard what they say about the hungry dead?"

"What if this is meant as some kind of sign?" I said. "You told us yourself that—"

Then, we heard a scraping at the door. Slow and careful. One scratch followed by another, down the length of the wood.

"He's found us," Peter said.

"Of course, He has. He's been in this room many times.

We've all taken supper here together." I moved toward the door to lift one of the chairs that barred it.

"What are you doing?" Peter said.

"I'm going to let Him in." I lifted another chair.

Peter shook his head. "You must not."

"What if He wasn't dead when we buried Him? What if He was merely weak? Now He stands out there all alone, needing our help."

"You told me your tunic was soaked in His blood," Peter said. "You told me the blood rained down on you."

It was true. I could still feel the heat of Yeshua's blood on my skin.

There was another scrape at the door.

Peter grabbed hold of my arm. "You were too close with Him, John. The two of you—the way you lay together—the way you touched. You aren't thinking clearly now."

I pushed Peter's hand aside. I'd been frightened when the shroud fell away in the tomb. But I knew I could not allow myself to be frightened any longer. This was Yeshua. My own Yeshua.

I unbarred the door and opened it.

He was there, naked. His eyes remained sealed. His jaw hung loose.

I backed away from the door, and Yeshua came into the room to stand before us.

I expected Peter to call out or even run, but he did not. I took Yeshua's hand. It felt cold like the earth. I turned the hand in mine, looking at the palm and the bones of the forearm. I examined the left side of His body and then the right. There were no wounds, though the Romans, in their terrible bright armor, had tortured Him for hours.

I attempted to guide Yeshua to one of the wooden chairs near the window. Whatever vague sense of reason I employed at that moment told me it might be good for Him to rest. But when I gently pulled at Him, His body would not be moved. He was like a heavy stone, permanent in its position. I touched His cheek. "Yeshua?"

He did not answer.

Gingerly, I began to pick the wax from his left eyelid. When the wax was gone, I raised the lid. The dark eye beneath was still His eye, but it did not focus on my face as it once had. Instead, it stared off into the distance. I picked wax from the other eye and raised the second lid. Then, I lifted His jaw with my index finger, closing His mouth, hiding His tongue. "Do you want something to eat, Yeshua?" I said.

He did not respond. Yet His body looked so frail. I had to try to feed Him.

I went to our cupboard, retrieving one of the small loaves of bread the women had baked for us. I broke the bread and attempted to give half of it to Yeshua. He did not take the bread. So I pulled a soft morsel from the loaf and put it in His mouth. The bread fell from His tongue to the floor.

†

PETER PACED THE room, watching as I washed the remnants of myrrh and oil from Yeshua's body with a wet cloth. I dressed Him in one of the woolen tunics we stored in a cedar box, and as I did, I noticed that Peter had squared his shoulders just as he used to when he spoke to our small group on the shores of Galilee. Some idea was taking shape in his mind. But I had no notion of what that idea might be.

In the past, Peter had often taken charge when Yeshua became confusing to us. After the long and curious speeches in the olive groves, for instance, Peter would ascend the mount and make sense of Yeshua's words. He claimed to act as translator. And everyone was thankful to him, though some had started to say privately that Yeshua was, in fact, Peter's own invention. Yeshua could make no meaning on His own. He spoke a kind of nonsense, telling of mysteries that lay beyond the desert. The others could not even remember most of the stories afterward. Yeshua remained a stranger. And Peter supplied a meaning that had not existed before.

After I'd dressed Yeshua, Peter went silently to one corner of the upper room where he kept a small supply of weapons. From the supply, he produced a black knife made of polished stone. I recognized the blade; he'd shown it to me once when we were boys, telling me the warlike men in the caves of Qumran had used it to sacrifice a sheep. "The sheep gave itself willingly," he said. "And Elohim was pleased."

At first, I thought Peter meant to harm Yeshua with his sacrificial knife.

I stepped between the two of them, unsure how I would thwart Peter's considerable strength. But instead of mounting an attack, he handed the black knife to me. "Use this if you must, John."

"Use it?"

"You're going to protect Him," Peter said.

"From what?"

"Everything that might want to harm Him."

"I don't understand," I said.

"You've told me yourself that you knew Him best. And it's true that He was always most comfortable with you at His side. Even now, He seems to take comfort in your presence."

Yeshua stared into one corner of the room with His newly opened eyes, seeming neither comfortable nor uncomfortable.

"What about the others?" I asked. "They will want to—"

"I'll explain this to them," Peter said. "And I'll tell them what we must do."

"Explain? But what will you say?"

"I'll make sense of it, John."

"But they'll want to see Him."

"No. No one would want to see this."

"We should tell them the truth," I said. "They deserve that."

Peter shook his head. "This cannot be the truth."

He moved to the door of the upper room and opened it. Then he turned to stare at Yeshua, as if he knew that Yeshua would want to leave. And, in fact, He did begin to walk.

So it was that I followed my friend and beloved out into the nighttime streets of Jerusalem, clutching the knife and a piece of bread, along with a bag I'd quickly gathered.

When we were some distance away from the old temple, I looked back at the stairs that led to the upper room. I wanted to take comfort in the lamps that burned there so warmly. But Peter had already closed the door against the darkness.

†

I FOLLOWED YESHUA down unpaved streets into the Lower City. Black houses of weathered limestone rose before us. The night was cold. The avenues, silent. Yeshua moved absently, a man asleep. But He was not asleep. The longer I followed Him, the more I began to feel as though He was in some state of utter absence. There was no sense of purpose in Him. No reason for any given step. We passed the Temple Mount and the Well of Souls. Yeshua walked along the inner wall of the city, sometimes brushing its stones with the sharp bone of His shoulder. By morning light, we'd left the city. We moved along the common road toward the foot of Mount Argaeus and the port city of Caesarea. Yeshua walked, and I followed, having hidden Peter's knife in the folds of my tunic so as not to raise alarm. We were a silent caravan, the two of us. When Yeshua attempted to board a ferrying ship at the port, I tried to stop Him, but found this was impossible. He would neither be moved nor halted. I paid one of the sailors for our travel. And as we set out, I saw writing scrawled onto one wall of the port: *Once you are dead, you are nothing.* I looked at Yeshua and wondered if such words might, in fact, be true.

†

HOW MANY DAYS did we spend on board the creaking vessel? It was impossible to tell. Time moved on an unsure foot in the rolling dark below the deck. None of the other passengers on board the ship spoke to us. Perhaps they sensed the bizarre nature of our situation. Yeshua refused to lay down beside me when it was time to sleep. And so, I curled myself at His feet like a dog whose master no longer cared for him.

When finally we disembarked the ship, I found, not a port city, but some assemblage of curious dark hovels gathered at the edge of the sea. Fires burned in common pits, filling the air with ash. There was no time to ask questions of the men who lingered about the pits, for Yeshua already made His way down an empty road that led out of the village. I followed Him, allowing Him, as always, to lead. He walked quickly at times, shuffling His feet. Then, for no apparent reason, He slowed. The sun began to set. Merchant caravans passed us on the road, bearing bolts of red silk and leather tanks of live horned fish. Men carried fragrant chests of cardamom and cinnamon. I spoke to Yeshua in a quiet voice, talking of the dust in the air, of Peter and Mary and all the rest. I told Him what had happened to Judas in the potter's field. I talked about the two of us, Yeshua and me. I thought something in these words, these memories might awaken Him, might make Him whole again. But He remained in His state of perpetual absence.

In the distance, a city soon rose, pillars red in the evening light.

I stopped a fellow traveler, an aged man with damp, rheumatic eyes. He walked with the aid of a heavy stick. I asked him the name of the city, and he looked, first at Yeshua and then at me, as if to determine the nature of our idiocy. "Where have you come from that you do not know what city that is?" he asked.

"Bethsaida," I said, "on the shores of Galilee."

"Well, that is Rome, boy," the old man said. Turning away, he added. "Best go back to your lake."

I found I could not speak. The arches and the temples, the great houses on the hill, all of it burned with the terrible fires of the evening sun.

Yeshua was already some distance ahead.

I called out to Him, begging Him to stop. But He did not even slow.

And so, I was forced to run, my hand already searching for Peter's knife.

†

The pale columns and towers of Jerusalem, the ancient shrines and hordes of men, all of it had once seemed almost impossible to me. So unlike the humble gathering of mud-brick houses where I'd spent my youth on the shores of Galilee. But Rome was nothing like Jerusalem. It was, in fact, no sensible place at all. As we passed beneath the southern gate, I felt as though we'd stumbled over the very edge of the world. Streets and lanes and crooked narrow footpaths, ramps of mud and clay, all of it spilled down on us at once. And we found ourselves, not on some stately avenue, but lost in a winding labyrinth of dark alleyways flanked by soot-stained tenements that rose like the black hives of insects. We walked on broken stone vessels and bloodied rags. A statue covered in vines and cinders appeared from the shadows like a monstrous herald. I followed Yeshua through the maze to a nearly empty street where shops were locked with sturdy bolts and thin rivers of dust trailed along the cobbles. I knew something of Rome's commerce, as an uncle on my father's side had once acted as a traveling merchant. He'd told us stories of the city, saying we should hope to never find ourselves in the streets of Rome at night. "Robbers and fiends of every sort move about," he said, "each of them searching for prey."

Yeshua stopped near a rude-looking fountain shaped like an oversized human head. Water trickled from the figure's mouth, running down its fat lower lip and into a stone basin below. I stood beside Him, attempting to make myself small. For though the street was largely empty, I did not want us to be marked. "You don't intend to stay here in this spot, do you?" I whispered.

Yeshua gazed absently at the fountain. The water was the color of iron.

Two Roman Legionnaires in long red capes turned a corner near us. I clutched Peter's knife against the folds of my robe. The soldiers were both powerful men, raked with muscle. I awaited their approach, their questions. I knew the terrible things they could do. But they barely glanced at us before moving on. And for the time being, I found I could breathe again.

†

NIGHT FELL AND the streets became like black canyons. Yeshua walked in what appeared to be an aimless manner, oftentimes causing us to circle back upon our own steps. The only lights we encountered were meager torches illuminating curious icons at crossroads. The icons were carved to look like the heads of humans and animals. I supposed their maker meant them as some manner of street marker. But they did nothing to alleviate my confusion.

At one point, a sallow man, half-naked, approached and held out his hands for alms. He bore an old wound in his cheek, through which I could see yellow teeth and a crusted tongue. I produced a coin from my purse and gave it to the man, hoping he did not have friends who would rob us.

At another juncture, a woman with hair dyed the color of flames approached. She wore layers of colorful shawls, and I assumed at first that she was a prostitute. But then she opened a wooden box and showed us a coil of three black snakes, adders by the look of them. She tried to sell the snakes to us, trailing us for a time, even though I indicated we did not want her animals.

After the woman departed, Yeshua and I came to a walled forest, a grove of thorny Ilex trees inside the city. The grove was likely a sacred place, as the garden wall bore carvings of winged gods, eyes bulging, mouths agape.

Yeshua entered the forest as if this had been His intended destination all along. Gardens had always pleased Him. And He seemed at home in this one.

He made His way toward the center of the grove where there stood a kind of altar, a block of marble with garlands draped about its edges. A number of apparent offerings lay upon the altar: stalks of wheat, a flagon of half-drunk wine. Blood streaked the marble. A sacrifice, I thought, performed rather recently, as the blood was still wet in places.

Yeshua stood before the offerings, and after a long while, I understood this was likely where He intended to spend the night. I touched His hand, hoping I might lead Him out of the garden, but He refused to move. Finally, I sat down at His feet, leaning my back against the altar. "Do you know where we are?" I asked. "This city?"

Yeshua did not reply.

"How do you not remember what they did to you?"

Again, no words.

"We aren't going to sleep here, are we? Out in the open? We have some money and—" But Yeshua had already turned away, staring off into the trees. I didn't bother to finish my thought. There was no possibility of argument. Yeshua would do as He would do.

I took His hand and tried to put it on my head. I wanted Him to stroke my hair as He once did. But as soon as I let go of the hand, it fell back against His side, and a tremendous sense of hopelessness washed over me. "I'm not going to let us die here," I said, though I did not know if I could rightly believe my own words.

†

IN THE NIGHT, I awoke. There was no moon, and the trees around us had become invisible. I'd heard voices in my sleep. Someone had come upon us. Thieves, I feared, or soldiers. I fumbled, once more, for Peter's knife. But even as I clutched its cold stone handle, I realized that, instead of moving closer to us, the voices moved further away, passing amongst the trees. I strained to listen to their words. A man and a woman recited a poem to one another.

"They lived like gods," the female voice said.

"Without sorrow of heart," the male replied.

"Miserable age rested not upon them."

"And when they died, it was as though they were

overcome with sleep."

The voices grew distant.

I wondered if the man and woman had performed the sacrifice at the altar earlier. Perhaps they now sealed their ritual with these incantations.

I found that I was too tired to contemplate their presence further.

As long as these phantoms didn't threaten harm, I would choose sleep over any investigation.

†

I NEXT AWOKE to morning light. Dew shone brightly on the Ilex trees. And, for the briefest of moments, I believed that everything would miraculously be as it should. Yeshua and I would find our way out of Rome. He'd awaken from whatever strange state imprisoned Him. And we would live out the rest of our lives together, tending sheep in some village near the sea. I turned to look for Him, hope still burning in my heart. But the hope fell to ashes as I saw He no longer stood beside the altar. There was, in fact, no sign of Yeshua in the clearing at all. I listened for the sound of His footsteps, but nothing rustled in the sacred forest. Cursing, I grabbed my pack and hurried toward the gate.

The Roman street looked unfamiliar in the bright light of morning. Slaves went about their errands while shopkeepers opened doors. I turned in a slow circle, searching for some sign of Yeshua. An aged fruit-seller glanced up at me as he set out baskets of walnuts and figs. A woman hanging bronze pots from the hooks in front of her shop sang a song in a language I did not recognize. Rome was full of foreign men: Egyptians and Ethiopians, Arabs and Thracians. Yeshua and I were merely two more foreigners here. And it seemed entirely possible that I'd lost Him forever to the vastness of the city. I wondered what Peter would say when I returned to Jerusalem alone. Certainly, he would berate me. But would he even truly care that Yeshua was gone?

Then, I caught sight of a familiar thin frame and a head of lank brown hair. Yeshua stood in the street some distance away. Yet rather than feeling triumphant that I'd found Him, I experienced a rush of panic, for two leather-capped Roman Legionnaires stood beside Him, appearing to ask questions.

I hurried toward the group, and the taller of the two guards glanced up at me. He was dressed in a short tunic and wore a purple cape held in place by a bronze pin. Engraved upon the pin was the image of a flame. The most curious thing about this guard was that his short-cropped hair was the color of new wheat. I'd encountered very few fair-haired men in my life, but enough to know they usually did not come from Rome. I couldn't imagine why such a man would be acting as a soldier here.

The shorter of the guards turned to look at me as well. He was the darker of the two men, olive-skinned. And, according to the frown he wore, he already didn't approve of me. "Does this one belong to you?" the shorter guard asked in Greek as he gestured toward Yeshua.

"My brother," I said. This wasn't exactly a lie. Peter often reminded us we were all brothers.

The shorter guard squinted. "Is your brother mute?"

"Since birth." This *was* a lie, but it couldn't be helped.

"Why are the two of you in Rome?" the shorter guard demanded.

"We're merchants," I said, thinking of my uncle. We've come to the city for—" I realized I didn't know any specific reasons that we, as merchants, might have come to Rome.

"Feralia?" the tall guard said. "Festival of the dead?"

"That's right." I replied, glancing at Yeshua with his hollowed cheeks and black-eyed stare. The irony of the festival's theme did not escape me. "We've come for Feralia." I looked at the tall guard with what I hoped was not too obvious an expression of thanks. He was handsome, yes, but hard-looking. He returned my gaze with the impassivity of a man made of marble.

"Well, you shouldn't let your brother wander off," the shorter guard said as he eyed Yeshua. "He's liable to get hurt. He limped up to us like a lost dog."

The fact that Yeshua had actually approached the two soldiers angered me. He was apparently attempting to invent new difficulties for us in an already impossible situation. "I won't let Him wander again. I promise you, I'll watch over Him." I took Yeshua's arm and said, "Come, brother."

But to my horror, Yeshua wouldn't move.

The guards watched with renewed interest.

"Is your brother unwell?" the tall guard asked.

"No. He's—" I searched for the right word in Greek as I wiped sweat from my brow. "Stubborn."

I wondered once again if there was some meaning to Yeshua's actions, some reason for His movements. He seemed particularly drawn to the pair of Roman guards. And because of that, we were all forced to wait.

Behind us, a voice called out sharply. It was the old shopkeeper, seller of walnuts and figs. A slave, a Syrian boy, had attempted to steal a piece of fruit. The shopkeeper now held the slave by the arm and called for the guards.

The tall guard nodded toward the shop, and the two of them made their way in the direction of the altercation without another word.

I stood before Yeshua, face hot with anger. "They could have hurt you," I said. "I am the one who saw such men hurt you before. Do you not remember that? I am the only one who saw."

Yeshua did not look at me. Instead, He stared at the basalt slabs imbedded in the street.

"We have to walk," I said. "We can't allow the soldiers to find us here when they return."

Surprisingly, Yeshua did walk then. And I hurried to follow.

†

WE PASSED A crowded street of booksellers where rolls of yellow papyri hung from wooden rods. Shopkeepers stood on boxes and read aloud in many languages. On the next street, perfume-makers displayed sweet-smelling wares in silver amphorae. Further on, we found a street of talismans: knotted cords, ampules filled with blood, and small figures in the shape of animals.

Before we could make it further, the tall fair-haired soldier emerged from a crowd on our left. I was so surprised that I almost didn't recognize him at first. But then I saw the flame engraved pin glinting in the sun. "Hold on, both of you," the soldier said, glancing behind him, as if to make sure he had not been followed.

"We're leaving," I said. "Just as you asked."

"It's not that." He set his jaw, flexing a muscle there. "My fellow watchman, called Magnus, believes now that he recognized your brother."

I nearly missed a step.

Yeshua kept walking, and I knew I could not afford to stop and listen to what this soldier had to say. I would not risk losing Him again. So instead, we all continued walking together. "What do you mean he *recognized* Him?" I said.

"From some skirmish," the tall solider said, "in the East."

"Your partner was—"

"In Jerusalem," the soldier said.

I blinked. "That's not possible."

"Your face tells me it *is* possible," the tall solider replied. "You don't need to explain. But my partner acted as though this skirmish was somehow memorable." He studied me with gray eyes. "You shouldn't be out in the open for a time. Magnus will drink wine this afternoon and he'll forget he saw you. Do you have somewhere to go?"

I didn't trust this soldier. For although he acted like he wanted to help, I'd seen firsthand how quickly such intentions could change. "We'll find a place," I said.

The soldier glanced over his shoulder again. "Continue ahead along this street. Don't circle back. You might run into Magnus. My name is Gallus by the way. May I know your name?"

"John," I said.

"And your brother?"

"He is—" I paused, "He's called Peter."

Part of me wanted to ask the soldier why he'd decided to warn us. But another part said I should spend no more time in his presence than necessary.

"Find shelter," Gallus said. "You'll discover there are many places to hide in Rome if you look for them."

†

YESHUA AND I walked in an unbroken line along the route, just as the soldier had indicated, and soon we arrived at a large piazza that appeared to serve as both meat market and butchery. Crowded tents and stalls spread before us. Spills of foul-smelling animal blood covered the travertine, and the air was thick with flies. We were far enough away from the square where we'd encountered the two soldiers that I thought we needn't worry about seeing Magnus or Gallus again. Yet, I also understood we could not be too careful. Yeshua made His way slowly through the crowds, as oblivious to any advice about finding a place to hide as He was to the shouts and bartering around us. At the market's center stood a sculpture done in blue-veined marble: the hero Theseus defeating the Minotaur. I knew the story well enough, as my mother, the displaced daughter of a Greek merchant family, often told such tales. She'd been unwell for many years, sick in her mind, eyes affected by the light of the sun. She secluded herself in a dark room and took to murmuring stories she'd heard in the kingdoms of her youth. She mixed rustic tales of Grecian gods with the stories of Abraham in a manner I'd found so confusing as a boy that I'd begun seeing all such stories as piles of dust. Nevertheless, I knew this Minotaur well enough. Head like a bull, the creature knelt in submission before the armored hero. Theseus gripped the Minotaur's horn, brandishing a sword. Yeshua stood near enough this display to make me think it might hold some meaning for Him. But soon, He moved on, showing no further interest.

I followed Him through narrow corridors of butcher's stalls, the crush of patrons and the coppery scent of blood. We came to a table stacked with goats' heads. Each ragged head studied us with clouded eyes.

Nearby, a muscular slave, naked but for a cloth between his legs, used a broad ax to butcher an ox. Gore covered both slave and ax. Two more slaves held the sides of the ox, attempting to keep the body upright. Blood poured from the animal. Everything, pierced and flayed. Everything spilling. The blood from the ox caused a rush of memory: the hill at Calvary, the bald and skull-like mount. The sky had been no color. The dirt of the hill was white with bone. Crosses stood broken, leaning. Roman soldiers in armor formed a circle around the cross, lifting spears and swords. I'd called out Yeshua's name, pushing forward through the crowd. His eyes rolled back. He opened His mouth.

Now, in the piazza, Yeshua turned toward me.

I expected to be greeted by the blank gaze that I'd grown so accustomed to. But something unexpected happened, an occurrence utterly remarkable. For the first time since He'd walked out of the tomb, Yeshua's black eyes appeared to focus on my face.

I approached Him, no longer aware of the market din, no longer concerned with the smell or the flies.

Yeshua continued to gaze at me. To actually *look* at me.

My heart pounded. "Are you awake? Have you—have you come back to me?"

He studied my face.

I felt the heat of tears. I stepped closer still. But His eyes did not move when I stood directly before Him. He was not looking at me at all. Instead, He gazed at something behind me.

I turned to see a large gray house in the distance beyond the market gates. It was not an apartment building, but rather what my uncle had once described as a "domus," a fine mansion of Rome's Old Republic. Yeshua stared not at me, but at the house.

"What is that place?" I asked.

Yeshua did not answer. Instead, He began to walk.

†

THE DOMUS WAS like an oyster, closed in upon itself, all gray walls and no windows. A curious knocker hung from the center of its heavy oaken door. The knocker, in the shape of a large bronze hand, appeared to have once clutched an object, something spherical, now missing. Yeshua stood before the door, swaying gently, as He had when Peter and I found Him in the tomb. I wondered briefly if I should knock. But I knew well enough Yeshua wouldn't be capable of speaking to the inhabitants. And I certainly had nothing to say. A man who owned such a house as this might very well call the guards if he perceived us as a nuisance or a threat. So instead of knocking, I waited, hoping Yeshua would move on. Yet, of course, He did not. Instead, He gazed fixedly at the door, eyes impossibly dark in the light of the afternoon sun.

There was no sound from inside the house, no clatter of life. To pass the time, I turned toward the street and absently watched as a sedan chair trundled by. A woman sat in the shade of the chair, veiled and reading from a scroll. A man walked behind her, leading a brown cat on a leash.

Then there came some Roman children, tossing a ball, shouting to one another. I soon began to feel frustrated by my inability to move away from the gray wall of the domus, and I attempted to ask a passing man about the place. The man, a slave by the look of his raw cloth tunic and shaved head, acted as though he didn't hear.

I tried again, asking two Roman noblemen. One of them was tall and lean, carrying a number of tablets under his arm. He'd used lampblack to fill in bald spots on his scalp. The other man was well-fed and carried an umbrella made of bone and red silk to shade himself from the sun.

The well-fed man didn't look at me when I spoke. Instead, he turned to his companion and said, "The Gray Palace draws the interest of every sort, does it not?"

The tall man nodded. "Every sort indeed. But good luck ever getting inside."

"Gray Palace?" I said. "Who does the palace belong to?"

The two moved on without response. I heard the well-fed man say: "I was told that poor old Vita tried to gain entrance again some weeks ago. The door did not open, of course."

"August too and Cassia. None of them permitted."

I turned to look back Yeshua. "The Gray Palace. Does that mean something to you?"

He stood, apparently transfixed.

"Just as I thought," I muttered.

†

HOURS PASSED, AND the heat of the sun became nearly unbearable as the walls of the Gray Palace provided no shade. I leaned against the house, sweat soaking my tunic. "We aren't going to leave this place, are we?" I said to Yeshua. "We're going to become withered old men here."

He continued to gaze at the door.

"Are you waiting for something?" I asked. "Or are you just stuck in the mud like a cow?" I wiped my brow. "That wasn't very kind of me. I'm sorry, Yeshua. I'll make a bargain with you. I'll knock on the door. But if some problem arises, we have to leave as quickly as possible. We'll lose ourselves in the market."

He gave no indication that He agreed or even understood.

I sighed and lifted the empty brass hand that hung at the center of the door. I used the hand to knock lightly, hoping there would be no answer. But only a moment passed before a previously invisible panel slid open in the door to reveal a small window.

I cursed under my breath as two green eyes appeared. The eyes belonged to a young woman, perhaps seventeen or eighteen. She wore makeup in a vaguely Egyptian style.

"Hello," she said.

"I'm sorry," I replied, lowering my head.

She blinked. "Sorry for what?"

"For disturbing you."

"You're not disturbing me," she said. "What gave you that idea?"

"Well—"

"I was a bit surprised, I suppose."

"I'm sorry to have surprised you then."

"It's just that we weren't due for any more visitors. But these kinds of things tend to happen for a reason, don't they? Would you like to come in?"

This casual invitation startled me, especially after what the two noblemen said about how difficult it was to gain access to the house. "No," I said. "We were just—"

Before I could finish my statement, the door opened, revealing the girl in full. She was dressed in an airy sleeveless garment and wore a ribbon, the color of sunrise, across her forehead. A gathering of buds from a honeysuckle plant was pinned in her dark hair. She smiled at us, a genuine smile. "You both look tired," she said, glancing at the street behind us. "The city is simply dreadful in the heat of the day, isn't it?"

"It is, I suppose."

"Well, why don't you come in off the street," she said, stepping aside so that we might enter the shaded hall. The corridor beyond was exceedingly plain, composed of large gray stones. A torch burned on one wall, dripping animal fat. The girl, in all her freshness, did not belong in such a funereal setting.

Before I could decline her invitation, Yeshua had already stepped inside. I considered grabbing His arm, but such an act would do no good. There was nothing to do but follow.

Once we were in the house, the girl closed the door behind us and locked it with a key. She put the key in a small leather pouch around her waist and seemed relieved to be sealed off from the bustling street. "Now," she said, clasping her hands and keeping her voice low, as if trying not to wake someone. "I assume you've come to see our Lady."

"Lady?" I said.

"That's the only reason anyone ever comes," she said. "But I'm afraid our Lady won't see you until later this evening. She told Jax that she won't see anyone before it's time. It might even be early tomorrow, depending on the circumstances of her preparations."

"Preparations?"

"That's right. For the celebration. Would you like a room? Somewhere to rest while you wait?"

The idea of a room in the safety of this fortress-like house appealed to me. The soldier, Gallus, had said we should hide ourselves away, and the house seemed the perfect place for that. "Is there a fee for the room?" I asked.

The girl raised her delicate brow. "Fee? Of course, not. Why would we charge for such a thing?"

"I'm not sure. Is it called the Gray Palace for a reason?"

Her smile faltered. "Oh, you mustn't say that. You seem like a nice enough young man. Our Lady will certainly think so. But you mustn't say things like that."

"Things like what?"

"This house doesn't have a name. Those on the outside

might have chosen one. We've heard that before. But—" She hesitated.

"I didn't mean offense," I said.

The girl's smile resurfaced. "You speak Greek with an interesting accent. Are you a farmer?"

"A fisherman."

"A fisherman!" she said. "What would it be like to catch a fish, I wonder?"

"It is...satisfying, I suppose," I said, though, in truth, I hated fishing. Whenever I found myself trapped on my father's boat, covered in guts and rocking in the waves, I wished I could be anywhere else. Anywhere at all.

The girl laughed. "I'm sure it's more than satisfying. Come, I'll show you where you can both rest."

She walked with a breezy step down the black corridor that led toward what I assumed was the rest of the house. Yeshua and I followed. There were moments when the shadows of the tunnel-like hall appeared to almost swallow the girl. If it were not for the sound of her footsteps, I might have believed she'd actually disappeared.

I took Yeshua's hand in the darkness. And though He did not grasp my hand in return, the mere presence of Him comforted me.

"What stone is this?" I asked, running one finger over the smooth walls of the black corridor.

"Obsidian, I believe," the girl answered from the darkness ahead. "Quarried from the depths of a volcano according to Jax. He's more knowledgeable about the natural world than I am."

"And who is Jax?"

"My brother. A twin. Born feet first. And because of that, I'm afraid he's quite a fool. But I still love him. We came here together from the island of Patmos. Our Lady summoned us. Jax had a dream."

"A dream?"

"That's right," she said as if it was the most natural occurrence in the world to be called to a house by a dream. "I'm Sapia, by the way. I'm sorry I didn't ask your name before."

"I'm called John."

"And your silent friend?"

"Peter," I said, growing more comfortable with this lie.

"John and Peter," Sapia laughed, as if there was some humor in this.

"Your brother had a dream that brought you here?"

"I might have had one too," Sapia said. "But I always forget my dreams. Even the important ones. Did you have a dream, John? Is that why you've come?"

"I didn't."

"Maybe your friend had one," she replied.

"Does everyone come to this place because of a dream?"

"Of course not. That would be ridiculous, wouldn't it? People come here for all sorts of reasons. Just like anywhere else."

From the tunnel-like hall, we emerged into a large stone atrium, the ceiling of which was open to the sky. A pool of blonde marble occupied the room's center, and the surface of the water reflected the rays of the afternoon sun. Light shimmered across the atrium's walls, revealing a fresco done in hues of emerald and gold. The scene the fresco depicted was set in a field of enormous white flowers. Painted petals folded one upon the next. And sprawled across the field were ten or twenty strong men, soldiers or sailors by the look of them. The men had not fallen in battle. Instead, they were in the thrall of a strange ecstasy. Many of them were naked, having cast off their armor. Some tasted the petals of the large flowers, as if the petals were a great indulgence.

"The Island of the Lotus-eaters," Sapia said, gesturing toward the fresco. "It's a story our Lady is quite fond of."

I tried to remember if I was familiar with the tale. Apparently, Mother had not told all the Greek stories. "Have these men gone mad?" I asked.

"Not mad," Sapia said. "They're filled up with—oh, I'm terrible at stories—*bliss*, I suppose."

I studied one of the men in the fresco. His eyes were wild, and he appeared to be drooling onto one of the oversized flowers. "Why does your Lady like this particular story?" I asked. "Is there some lesson to be learned?"

"She doesn't like lessons," Sapia said. "Quite the opposite, in fact." She glanced at Yeshua who stood near the fresco, not looking at the scene but staring indiscriminately in the direction of the reflecting pool. "Your friend...is he always this quiet?"

"That's His way," I said.

"Our family knew such a man on Patmos," Sapia replied. "He was always considering some point of philosophy. When he finally found he had something to say, he would say it. And he'd say the most glorious things. But, in the meantime, we often forgot he could speak."

"I suppose my friend is a little like that too." I often wished that others could have witnessed Yeshua telling His stories in the olive groves outside Jerusalem. Even if we had not always understood His meaning, the way He spoke had so compelled us.

Sapia led us toward the back of the atrium to a series of arched marble doorways that opened onto a series of sleeping chambers. Each chamber door was curtained with a fine, nearly-transparent muslin. Lamps burned inside the cell-like rooms, revealing supine figures on wooden pallets. The figures were all in a state of restful sleep. Such a state appealed to me greatly after having spent the night on the uneven, brambled floor of the sacred forest.

"Would you and Peter like separate rooms?" Sapia asked.

"One will do," I said. "But might I ask—"

Sapia turned, her eye makeup shining in the light.

"What is the purpose of this place? Is it some kind of boarding house?"

She laughed. "A boarding house? Does it look like a boarding house?"

"You have rooms," I said. "As well as men and women sleeping."

"It's not a boarding house, John. Or a tenement or a House of Venus or anything of the sort. This is a place where people can truly rest."

"It seems quite peaceful," I said.

"Peaceful is the least of it," Sapia replied. "It's absolutely restorative. I remember the first night I spent in this house. Jax and I were so weary from our travels that we could barely stand upright when we arrived. I thought it would take us weeks to recover, especially in the chaos of Rome, but the next morning I awoke with more vitality than I had ever known. Jax told me about the work we were to do here, and I found myself tremendously excited to begin."

"What work was that?" I asked.

"The organization of the house," Sapia said. "We were to become its stewards."

"You still haven't fully explained the house's function."

Sapia took a breath. "Our Lady will explain it better than I could. Even my brother would have more to say. He's a bit of a philosopher too, I suppose. Let me just leave you to your sleep for now. I'm sure the meaning of the house will be made apparent soon enough."

†

THE ROOM SAPIA granted us was so welcoming, so entirely a place of comfort, that I soon forgot any confusion about the house or its nature. The clean raised palette and small wooden table reminded me of the room Yeshua and I had once shared on the shores of Galilee, the room where I had so often whispered my devotions. A jug of wine and a wooden cup sat on the table in the corner, and I thought of how we sometimes drank wine together and talked late into the night. Or rather, I talked and Yeshua listened. This seemed always to be the way of things. I told Him of my mother and her illness. I told Him of my father and the sea and how lonely I felt amongst the other men. I told Him too that I was glad I would never have to feel lonely again. Then I would kiss His delicate wine-stained lips, and He would kiss me in return.

In the Gray Palace, Yeshua stood beside the table, gazing at the wall. His body was still with me. That much was true. And yet, Yeshua Himself, His essence, was no longer there. Because of that, I felt more alone than ever before. I sat on the palette, and attempted to rest. I'd been so vigilant since we left Galilee, barely daring to ever close my eyes. "This was not a bad choice," I said to Yeshua. "If you did choose it, that is." I wished, in that moment, that He would turn and look at me, that He would come to sit with me on the palette and put His arm around me. He would say: "You only had to trust in me, John." That is what Peter often said. We must trust in Yeshua. And we would lay together as we once had. Finally, I could feel at peace. But, of course, there was no chance of that.

Instead, I reclined on the palette, closing my eyes, hoping I might fall asleep. Yet sleep did not come, and I found myself thinking once more about the great house where we found ourselves. My uncle had told me once that, although Rome was dangerous in many ways, there were also fine things to see. Some of the finest wonders in the entire world, in fact. He'd once attended a dinner at the house of a nobleman where he'd seen a great volcano made of ice. Oysters and squid eggs filled the frozen crater at the volcano's center. Slaves served wine mixed with honey, and before the main course, they cut open the blackened belly of a roasted boar to release some twenty *living* songbirds.

The idea of such a banquet fascinated me. For much of my childhood, I believed the only marvels I'd ever see were the weathered riggings of the fishing boats of Galilee.

Soon, I found my curiosity getting the better of me. I was still a young man, after all. And I could not always contain my desires, much to Peter's chagrin. If there was to be a celebration in the house, as Sapia had said, perhaps some of the wonders my uncle had described might already be on display.

I sat up, looking at Yeshua, who continued to stand perfectly still near the small table. "I'd like to look around," I said. "Just for a moment. You can come if you like."

Yeshua continued to stare at the wall in silence.

"All right. But you can't go wandering. You have to promise me that you won't."

He did not move from His spot. And I supposed that, in itself, was something of a promise. The truth of the matter was that the house seemed like quite a safe place for Yeshua. Sapia had locked the front door, and even if He decided to move, I didn't think He could get far.

†

To begin my brief exploration, I thought I might speak with one of the men or women lying on palettes in the quarters adjacent to our own. Perhaps they would be able to explain the Gray Palace better than Sapia. But when I gazed at the figures through the sheer curtains of their rooms, I saw again how peaceful they appeared. To pull them from the cradle of their dreams would be unkind. So instead, I decided to wander on my own, not toward the entrance of the house, but into deeper regions. I'd tucked Peter's black knife into the belt of my tunic, concealing its blade in the folds of fabric at my waist, just in case something untoward happened. This was Rome after all.

At the back of the atrium, I discovered a wide door flanked by two fluted columns. The triangular pediment over the door bore an inscription in a language I could not read.

I stepped through the doorway, and having done so, discovered that I suddenly stood in what appeared to be the depths of a great forest lit only by the full moon that hung in a cloudless sky above a dense gathering of trees.

Finding myself outside was startling enough. But more surprising still was the fact that the hour had grown so late. For when Yeshua and I had entered the house, the sun had barely passed its midpoint. And although we'd spent a relatively short time in our quarters off the atrium, somehow, here in the forest, night had fallen.

I looked back at the open doorway through which I'd

just passed and saw that the atrium was, in fact, still bright. The rays of the afternoon sun fell softly upon the blonde marble pool.

Confused, I turned back toward the forest and peered up at the moon that hung in the nighttime sky. After a moment's further observation, I realized it was no moon at all. Instead, it appeared to be some sort of clever device, a pocked and reflective surface, perhaps made of copper, mounted near the black ceiling of a vast, dark chamber. The light of a hidden lamp shone upon the surface of a metal plate, making the moon glow.

As soon as I understood that this moon was, in fact, a false thing, I wondered how I'd been deceived in the first place. For though the device was clever enough, the illusion was a poor counterfeit. Nothing like the actual moon. And yet, it *had*, for the briefest of moments, been the moon to me.

My uncle had been right about Roman houses. They were indeed filled with wonders. I wanted to see something more of what this house had to offer. And thinking of Yeshua alone in our room, I decided He would be safe for a short while longer. I walked deeper into the grove and realized that, unlike the moon, the trees of the forest were quite real. I smelled the mossy damp of them and recognized varieties of Myrtle and Acanthus. The trees grew up through spaces cut into the stone floor. There must have been soil beneath. And at some point, the trees must have received the light of the sun. I had no idea why the owners of the house would have gone to all the trouble of planting a forest inside a room however. Clearly, they had strange predilections.

The faint sound of a footstep came from somewhere to my left, and I turned to see a man in a carefully pleated white toga standing at the base of a Cypress tree. He gazed at the tree in a state of apparent contemplation. "Hello?" I said.

He appeared startled. He was somewhere near middle-life, with a high brow and a finely trimmed beard that had not yet grayed. His cheeks were pinkish and his eyes, almost too bright. "Who's there?" he said, peering into the darkness. He spoke sharply, and I thought I might have made a mistake calling out to him.

"I am called John," I said.

"How did you get in here, John?"

I wondered if he might be the master of the house, perhaps related in some way to the mistress Sapia had spoken of. "I came from the atrium." I gestured in the direction of the door through which I'd recently passed. Trees now obscured it.

"Atrium?" the man said.

"My friend and I were just admitted by the young woman."

"What woman?" he asked.

"Sapia is her name," I said.

This aristocrat considered this and said finally, "There was no young woman."

"But I just met her."

He shook his head. "It was a young man."

"Her brother," I said. "She spoke of him. They're twins."

The man appeared unsure. "I am called Regulus Aulus Pius," he said. "My father was the senator Regulus Scipio Pius. He died recently of a wasting disease. And I feared I might develop the same condition myself. I came here to this house because I'd heard of its restorative properties. But instead of feeling restored, I find myself now—confused."

"Confused?"

"Come look at this tree, boy," Regulus said.

I went to stand beside him.

"Now, tell me what you see."

I studied the shallow ridges of the fibrous hide. "I suppose I see tree bark."

"Look closer now."

I leaned closer to the tree. "What am I looking for, sir?"

"Do you see *words*, boy?"

"Words?"

"That's right. Not carved into the bark, but appearing to grow naturally there."

I shook my head. "There are no words." I wondered then if this man might be mad in a manner similar to my mother.

Regulus peered at the tree. "The words must be on another tree," he said. "There were instructions. I saw them earlier." He turned to me. "Which way is this atrium you speak of?"

"There." I gestured toward the copse of trees behind us.

He looked in the direction I pointed. "Why are you

trying to deceive me, boy?"

"There's a door," I said. "Just beyond the trees."

Regulus's expression soured further. "If I go beyond the trees and I do not find a door, I will blame you. I'll remember your face."

"How long have you been wandering, sir?"

"I have to go," he said. "There's to be a celebration. And I have to join the others before it begins. I was hoping the words in the trees would help me along."

"Might I ask what you're celebrating?"

But Regulus did not answer. Perhaps he did not hear.

†

The deeper I walked into the great dark room, the more I began to feel as though I was in an actual forest again. The painted ceiling became the nighttime sky, and the round copper plate suspended above the trees was once more the moon. For a few moments, I even believed I heard the low and distant hum of an insect's song. How these illusions regained their power, I cannot say. But I will admit my confusion was not entirely unpleasant. A certain curiosity rose in my breast. And I was reminded of a similar feeling I'd experienced when, as a boy, I went wandering in the arid desert beyond our village. I was small at the time, and I crawled under a table and then along the floor until I escaped my mother who was busy preparing food. This happened in the years before she began closing herself off in a dark room and mumbling stories of the old gods. I walked slowly in the hot sun, following a small brown snake for a time because I was interested in its odd, curling gestures. Soon, I realized I was far from the village. I could barely see the gathering of white shelters on the horizon. But I did not feel afraid. Instead, I gazed out over the rocks and sand, sensing the impossible openness of the landscape. In that moment, part of me believed that the desert did not end. It stretched on forever in all directions. But another part of me (one that spoke in a voice I did not recognize) said: *Of course, the desert ends, John. Just as everything ends. The mountains, the sea, the lives of men.* I'd recently witnessed an old fisherman die in the street near my father's house. He'd fallen in the dust, clutching his stomach, and though several men tried to help him, the old man howled in pain until his voice simply stopped. One of the men said, "He is dead." And at first, I was frightened. Perhaps I even began to cry because soon my father appeared beside me and said: "Do not worry, John. That man is lucky. Now he knows all there is to know." I thought of what my father said as I gazed out over the desert. I wanted to travel deeper that day, to know the limits of the landscape. Because, even as a boy, I believe I understood that to find a limit was to gain a certain power.

†

I REALIZED THAT if I walked a straight line through the false forest of the Gray Palace, I would eventually come to a wall. There had to be a wall because this was, in fact, a room. Cavernous, yes, but still undeniably a room. So I made my way directly along a chosen path, touching trees as I walked, as if marking their trunks with my hands. I wondered again about what Regulus had told me—that he'd seen words in the bark of the trees. Not carved there but somehow manifesting naturally. I had no idea what such a thing might mean. And I told myself it probably didn't matter as it was likely nothing more than a product of the nobleman's overall confusion. After walking for some time, I came to a stone wall painted as black as the nighttime sky. And using the wall as my guide, I made my way around the room's perimeter. Soon, just as I'd predicted, I found a door cut into the stone. And I felt a certain pride at having discovered the limits of this space, as well as feeling a moment of pity for poor, confused Regulus.

Passing beneath the arch of the door, I found myself no longer amongst the trees, but inside what appeared to be a dim-lit amphitheater. Wide stone steps led down to the semi-circle of a stage. The back of the stage resembled a pillared and graven forum. Burning sconces cast an eerie glow over the entire edifice, as if some tragedy was about to begin. Yet the theater and the stage were empty. Or at least that's how they appeared at first.

As I studied the stage's facade, however, a human figure began to take shape in the shadows. The figure looked to be that of a wiry young man seated between two pillars. His legs were crossed and drawn, and a garment made of feathers covered his shoulders and arms, giving him the appearance of having wings. On his face, he wore a mask with a long beak-like snout. And his fingers were laced beneath his chin as if he was lost in thought.

I took a step toward the stage and heard what I assumed was the young man's voice. His tone was not threatening, but clear. "Please," he said, "don't come any closer."

I stopped on the steps.

"Have a seat if you like," he said.

Unsure what else to do, I lowered myself onto one of the wooden benches.

The young man resumed his silent meditation, and I wondered if all of this might be part of some rehearsal. Finally, he cleared his throat and spoke in the manner of an orator reciting a text from memory: "'While everyone else is laughing and drinking,'" he said, "'you extend a surreptitious claw toward the table napkins of the negligent.'" He cleared his throat again. "'An unattractive habit you misguidedly think is funny.'" Then he looked up at me through the eye-holes of his bird mask, waiting for a response.

"What was that?" I asked.

"Catullus," he said. "A poet of some renown. What did you think?"

"It didn't sound much like poetry."

He nodded. "I'm fairly certain that's the point." He

adopted the awkward oratorical tone once more. "'No sooner had I kissed you than—with every finger, in every corner of your mouth—you washed and rubbed all contact of my lips, like the slaver of some syphilitic whore.'" He looked up at me.

I felt more than a little uncomfortable. "I don't know anything about poetry," I said.

The young man's sigh echoed off the amphitheater's walls. "A fellow novice," he said. "I myself am trying to learn before—well—just *before*. I don't recognize you by the way."

"I only just arrived."

"Really? Did my sister let you in?"

"The young woman. Sapia."

"That would be my sister," the young man said.

"You're Jax?"

"Eternally." He tapped the forehead of his mask in a quick salute. "It's odd though. We weren't supposed to let anyone else into the house." Jax raised his mask and rested it on his brow. His features were sharp, almost avian, with thick black eyebrows that connected in the middle above the severe beak of a nose. He gazed up at me in the dim light. "Ah, I see why she let you in."

"Why is that?"

"Because you're—pretty," he said, half-smiling. "In a countryish manner. Unkempt hair. The glow of the sun upon your cheeks. And you look foreign too. Sapia likes foreign men." Jax shrugged. "Not that she'd ever do anything about it. She doesn't think there's time."

Being called "pretty" did not exactly sit well with me. Peter had sometimes called me such things when he was in one of his less than agreeable moods. "I'm not from Rome," I said.

"That much is evident," Jax said. "Entertain my curiosity for a moment, country boy. Do you take carnal interest in men or women?"

I tried not to register my further discomfort. I'd heard Romans were even more permissive than Greeks. Yet this seemed a significant indiscretion.

"There's no point in being shy," Jax said. "Especially not in this house. What's your name?"

"I am called John."

Jax smiled again and, deepening his voice, said, "*I am called John*. Very formal, aren't you, John?"

"I suppose I am."

"I see. Well, if you're not from Rome, where exactly do you hail from?"

"A village on the shores of Galilee."

"Gala—" Jax said, as if the word didn't quite fit in his mouth.

"Galilee."

"Never heard of it."

"It's—"

He gestured dismissively. "Don't worry. I come from somewhere no one's ever heard of as well. *Pat*-mos. Embarrassing, honestly. There aren't even any stories told about the island. No gods ever walked there or heroes. If you go in for that sort of thing." He hesitated. "Do you go in for that sort of thing?"

"Gods?"

"And heroes," Jax said. "Handsome and doomed."

"My mother told Greek stories," I said. "Another fisherman in my village, Peter, tells stories too. But I don't put much stock in them."

"Fascinating," Jax said. "At any rate, I'm glad to be away from Patmos myself. Sapia misses the old place. But I definitely do not. A lot of primitives there. Men wailing and beating each other with sticks. And the people believe in every sort of demon and sprite imaginable." Jax sighed. "Have you been to the baths, John?"

"Baths?"

"A custom here in Rome. There's the caldarium. That's the hot bath. And the frigidarium. That's the cold one. I've heard it's all quite stimulating, dipping oneself in and out of the waters."

"I haven't been many places in Rome," I said.

"Nor I, sadly," Jax said. "Sapia and I have more than a few duties here at the house." He adjusted the gray feathers on his shoulders. "So, John, let's try this again: men or women?"

"Why do you keep asking me that?"

He shrugged. "Seems as good a question as any, doesn't it? It's compelling at least."

It did not, in fact, seem compelling. It was the sort of

question that had hovered like some specter between my father and me for my entire life. Never spoken out loud, of course, and somehow all the more damning because of that. The question had lurked in shadows between me and the other fishermen too. And the answer had seemed both known and unknown simultaneously. Only Peter had ever spoken of my desires directly and always with such disgust. Peter who believed he understood me entirely, that he could draw a circle and contain me. "Which do you prefer?" I asked Jax.

"Oh, most definitely men," he replied without hesitation. He removed his bird mask and set it beside him on the stage, revealing black hair that stood in short spiked whorls. "Women are fine when it comes to a poet's inspiration. But they're not the sort I'd want to, well, you know... Now, your turn."

"I don't feel comfortable answering," I said.

"Ah," Jax replied.

"What?"

"Well, that clearly means you're interested I men."

"I think I should go," I said.

"Go? Where are you going to go?"

"Back to my friend. He needs me."

"Oh," Jax said.

"He shouldn't be left alone too long."

"No?"

"He's not well." I stood and started to walk back up the stairs.

"It doesn't matter if your friend is unwell," Jax said. "Or, I should say, it won't matter for long."

"Why wouldn't it matter?"

"Because things are about to get a bit more *difficult* in the house," Jax said. "And once things become more difficult, no one's going to be thinking about who's ill and who's not and that sort of thing."

"What do you mean?"

"My sister had her reasons for letting you in, I'm sure," he said. "But she should have explained the circumstances more clearly, I'm afraid."

"What are the circumstances?"

"There's to be a celebration," Jax said.

"So you all say. But no one will tell me the cause for the celebration."

"It's good you met me then, isn't it, John?" Jax said. "I always tell the truth. No matter how troubling that truth might be. It's a philosophy that's gotten me in some trouble over the years."

"What sort of trouble?"

"I'd rather not talk about that," Jax said.

"But you said you always tell the truth."

"There's a difference between lying and not wanting to talk about something. You should know that as well as anyone with your, 'I don't feel comfortable answering.'" Jax adjusted his feathers. "And no one is likely to tell you anything about the celebration. They all feel rather conflicted because 'celebration' is the wrong word."

"What's the right word?"

"Ritual?" Jax said. "Or sacrifice? That's what our Lady intends."

"She's performing a sacrifice?"

"Correct."

"What's to be sacrificed?"

He smiled faintly, though I could not tell if the smile meant he was pleased or vaguely unnerved. "Well, there's a bit of confusion about that too, I'm afraid. But, as I said, I think things are going to be rather more difficult here in the house after the celebration begins."

"Who is this Lady?"

"I can't tell you that," Jax said. "Mainly because I'm not exactly sure. She traffics in what some might call mysteries."

"But she summoned you here," I said.

"That's right."

"So you must know something about her."

"Not necessarily."

"Well, I don't want any part of her mysteries," I said.

Jax rested his head against a stone pillar. "You should probably leave then. Though that might prove to be somewhat of a problem."

"Why would it be a problem?"

"I'm assuming the front door is locked," Jax said.

"Your sister has the key," I replied.

He sighed. "Unlikely."

"I saw her put it in a pouch she wears at her waist."

"Our Lady will have demanded the key by now. She won't want it just floating about. Especially not when the celebration is so close at hand."

"Is there some other way out?"

Jax leaned forward. "There is."

"Tell me."

"There's another door. At the rear of the house. But you would have to go through quite a lot of trouble to reach it. I doubt it's worth—"

"But it's unlocked?"

Jax nodded. "There's no lock on that door. The house is like the god, Janus. Have you heard of Janus?"

"I—"

"Two faces," Jax said. "Each staring in different directions. So you could try to find the other door. Or you could just stay here with me."

"Don't you want to leave?"

"I can't," Jax said. "I'm in this. Part of it." He raised his feathered arms, showing off the costume. "Sapia and I are protected though. Our Lady has promised us as much. We're the caretakers, the stewards. If you want to leave, you should probably hurry. The celebration will begin soon. Only a matter of hours left, I should think."

I turned to go.

"And John," Jax called from behind me. "You'll want to watch out for my sister. She's a lovely girl, but she really takes all this to heart. Quite a disciple of our Lady, I'm afraid. Just be careful, won't you?"

†

I SKIRTED TREES that glowed with false moonlight, all the while cursing myself for allowing us to become ensnared in this certainly queer and possibly dangerous predicament. I attempted to cut through the center of the forest, assuring myself that the door to the atrium wouldn't be difficult to find. Yet, soon enough, I was forced to stop in a grove near a flowing stream and admit that nothing in the forest looked familiar to me. The branches of the trees that circled the grove cast odd crooked shadows over the ground, a pattern that appeared to form a series of runic figures. I thought of Regulus, the senator's son. He too believed there were symbols in the trees. He'd become confused in the forest, wandering aimlessly. I couldn't allow myself to fall into the same trap. What had seemed an almost pleasant illusion before now felt like a threatening maze. The forest separated me from Yeshua. And it kept us from our freedom. I wondered how I'd been so foolish as to believe any place in Rome was safe. This house was proving to be like one of my father's eel traps, easy enough to get into, but far more difficult to escape.

I took a breath and turned in a slow circle, focusing on the spaces between the trees. I reminded myself that this was no forest and it did not go on forever. I needed only to do what I'd done before—choose a specific direction and walk in a straight line until I found the wall that enclosed the room. I could follow the perimeter back to the atrium door. This would take more time of course but it was, at least, a certainty.

As I walked, I felt suddenly that someone might be watching me from the cover of the trees, perhaps assessing my ability to negotiate this puzzle. I turned and said, "Who's there?" wondering if it might be Regulus, still lost. Or even Jax in his bird feathers, come to find me, to ask me more questions. But there was no response. And so, I hurried on. The sensation of being watched passed quickly enough. And I decided that, even if there was a watcher, I must pay him no mind. I couldn't allow any sensation to knock me off my course.

Soon, I found the black perimeter wall, just as before. I touched its surface as if to verify the existence of the stone. And then I began to follow the wall, sliding my hand along, imagining how I would gather Yeshua once I arrived at our room. We'd make our way toward the back of the house together, to the exit Jax had promised. I didn't know why Yeshua had brought us to this house. But I understood now that we most certainly needed to leave.

I stopped only once more in the forest. And it was during that pause that I imagined Peter scowling at me from the shadows of the trees. This sort of waking dream was not an unusual occurrence. I had a habit of imagining conversations with Peter, even though I knew such exercises could have no positive effect. For a time, I'd worried that my hallucinations indicated I'd inherited my mother's madness. But the truth of the matter was that Peter had made such a strong impression upon me at a young age that his voice had lodged itself in my brain like the tip of a poisonous spear.

"How exactly did you become so stupid?" the imagined Peter asked from his place between the trees. I could see him there in the shadows. He wore the tattered brown tunic of his youth, cinched with a length of fisherman's rope. "Did your Greek mother drop you on your head?"

"I'm not stupid," I whispered.

"Perhaps she didn't drop you then. But she did make you what you are, you know."

"What am I?"

"I don't have to explain that," Peter said. "You know well enough. Apparently, the young man in the theater knew as well."

"I don't need you in my head right now."

"How are you going to get out of this house if I'm not here to tell you what to do?" he asked. "How are you going to get *Him* out of the house?"

"I'll find a way."

"You're not terribly clever if I remember correctly from the games of our youth."

"I'm not as foolish as you imagine, Peter."

Yet when I arrived at our sleeping quarters off the atrium, I realized I was wrong about what I'd said. The truth of the matter was, I was very foolish indeed. For my leather satchel lay scattered on the floor near our pallet. And Yeshua was nowhere to be found.

My heart raced. He was gone, and His disappearance was most certainly my fault. I'd allowed the house to put me under some spell. What had I been thinking, wandering off like that?

I backed out of our quarters, turning toward the chamber closest to our own. The occupant of the room lay stiffly upon his pallet, still sleeping. "Sir?" I said, approaching the gauze curtain that hung across his door. "I'm wondering if you might...have you seen my friend?"

The man didn't respond. In fact, he remained entirely still.

It occurred to me, in that moment, that the man might actually be dead.

Perhaps the mysterious Lady of the house had already begun the ritual Jax had described.

Perhaps she'd brought harm to Yeshua as well.

I drew back the room's curtain and stepped inside. There was a strong odor in the air. And though it was not the stench of death, it was disquieting nonetheless. For the room smelled inexplicably of wildflowers. Not a few flowers, but an entire lush field of them. I could see the field in my mind's eye, white Crocuses and purple Mandrake, a prickle of Roman Nettle. And yet there were no actual flowers in this room.

"Sir?" I approached the man who lay on his back, arms at his sides. He wore a gray tunic and a curious medallion—a small open hand made of copper. Its shape was the same as the hand of the doorknocker. The man appeared Roman with hawkish features and short clipped hair. His eyes were closed.

I got to my knees and put my ear to his mouth. His breath was warm against my skin. He was alive, at least. But as I studied his face more closely, I perceived a troubling detail. Some kind of thin gray plant-matter covered the man's lips, a variety of mold or fungus. And I wondered if the man had been poisoned. Perhaps somehow by flowers?

I put my hand on his shoulder, preparing to shake him.

"John?" a female voice said from the doorway.

At first, I thought it might be the Lady of the house. But then, I turned and saw Sapia peering through the gauze. She carried a wooden tray of food—unleavened bread, dates, and a small container of honey. She looked at me with concern.

"What are you are doing to Master Drusus?" Sapia asked.

"Where is Yesh—" I began and stopped myself. "Where is Peter?"

"I thought you were both resting," Sapia said. "I brought food."

"He's not in our room. And someone has gone through my things."

"That can't be." Sapia cast a troubled glance toward our room. "This is a safe place. One of the safest in all of Rome. Maybe it was your friend who looked through your belongings."

"No," I said. "He didn't."

"How do you know?"

"Because He takes no interest in...material possessions."

She took a step closer. "Tell me what you were doing to Master Drusus."

"I was checking to make sure he was still alive," I said.

"Alive?"

"He doesn't wake when I speak to him."

"That's because he's resting."

"This isn't rest," I said.

She looked at me as if I was a child. "It's a different sort of rest. He's preparing for—"

"Don't say the celebration."

"But he *is* preparing for the celebration. We all are."

"Your brother told me what's really happening here," I said.

Sapia raised a thin eyebrow. "You spoke with Jax?"

"I did."

"Wherever did you find him?"

"The theater," I said. "He told me that there's to be a ritual. The celebration is some kind of sacrifice."

Sapia blinked. "Jax said that?"

"What is to be sacrificed, Sapia?"

She shook her head. "I'm sorry, John. The truth of the matter is that Jax can be quite cruel. Not to me, of course. He's always been kind to his sister. But he's cruel to others. And he's especially cruel when he's bored. Our Lady is already displeased with him. And when she discovers he's in the theater again *and* telling lies—well—she'll likely punish him."

I narrowed my gaze. "He was lying?"

"Jax doesn't consider it lying," Sapia said. "In his mind, he's telling a story, like the poets do. He's always acted this way. Ever since we were children. He stages little dramas involving people who have no idea what he's up to. You became part of his show, his epic-in-miniature, I'm afraid." She paused. "I sometimes wish he hadn't come with me to Rome. But it was Jax who had the dream, of course."

"Sapia," I said. "I need you to tell me where my friend is. Where is Peter?"

"I've already told you. I don't know. I thought—"

I didn't wait for her to finish. I stood and passed through the curtain, moving out into the atrium.

Light from late afternoon sun glittered on the water of the reflecting pool. The soldiers in the great fresco continued to loll in eerie ecstasy, eating from the large pale flowers.

I thought of the floral scent in Master Drusus's room and wondered if I'd somehow been smelling lotus flowers there.

Sapia followed me into the atrium and set the tray of food down on a small table near the pool. "You mustn't get too excited," she said. "Your friend is here somewhere. I'm sure of it."

"Peter is important to me, Sapia," I said. "I take care of him."

"I understand that," Sapia said.

"No," I said, "you don't."

She cast her eyes downward, as if I'd hurt her feelings.

"Is it possible He's been led out onto the street by someone?" I asked. I walked down the dark stone hall that opened onto to the entryway. Sapia followed. I reached the front door of the house and attempted to turn the handle but found it locked, just as Jax had predicted. "Open the door. I want to make sure He isn't outside."

"John," Sapia said. "You friend isn't on the street."

"How do you know?"

"Because—"

"Open the door, Sapia."

"I can't."

"What do you mean?" I said.

"You mustn't raise your voice. People are trying to rest. If you wake them, well—I cannot predict what will happen."

"I don't care if people are trying to rest. Tell me why you can't open the door."

"Our Lady," Sapia said.

I turned and saw that the leather pouch around Sapia's waist where she'd deposited the key was indeed gone. Jax had been correct about this turn of events as well.

"And why would your Lady prevent you from opening the door?"

"Because her celebration is of a delicate nature," Sapia said. "It must be performed in the correct manner and in the right environment. All of the necessary participants are already gathered here in the house."

"Master Drusus is a participant?" I asked.

"That's right," Sapia said.

"And the man I met in the forest, Regulus, he is a participant as well?"

"I didn't know you met Regulus," Sapia said. "He's a very nice man."

"And do you imagine that *we* are somehow to be participants?" I asked. "Peter and me?"

"I'm terribly upset with Jax for frightening you," she said. "I'm going to have a talk with him. I promise. I'll tell him to correct this somehow. He must stop being so cruel to our guests."

"Where is the person you call your Lady?" I asked. "I want to talk to her."

"I told you she won't be available until later this evening or even tomorrow morning, John. She's very busy at the moment."

"If we don't find Peter soon," I said. "I'm going to wake everyone in the house, and I'll ask them where He's gone. I'll make so much noise that—"

Sapia raised her hands as if to cover her ears. "Oh, don't say that. Please...I'll help you find your friend. But please don't talk like that."

"Help me then," I said.

She appeared honestly distressed. "I have an idea about where he might be. Follow me."

†

SAPIA LED ME back through the hall of volcanic rock to the painted atrium. The skylight revealed large clouds passing above. The city of Rome still existed just beyond the walls of the Gray Palace, yet nothing had ever seemed more remote to me. Sapia, for her part, paid no attention to the clouds. Instead, she went to the great fresco of the lotus-eaters and touched one of the white blossoms painted there. The gesture appeared, at first, to be a kind of caress, as if Sapia, like the sailors, sought pleasure from the flowers. But then, the petal that Sapia touched slid back into the wall, releasing the latch of a hidden door. The door swung open to reveal a winding staircase leading down. Torches burned in stone sconces, casting tendrils of light across the stony wall.

"There is a catacomb beneath the house," Sapia said, "It was once used to store wine. But now the catacomb is empty. The door was open earlier as we made our preparations. It's possible your friend wandered down the stairs."

I was surprised at how reasonable this sounded. Yeshua was indeed prone to wandering. And if the door had been open, it was entirely possible that He might have made his way down.

I followed Sapia into the catacomb. Dim arched hallways led in three directions from a central chamber. A few broken wine flasks were stacked in one corner of the otherwise empty space.

"Is your Lady in the catacomb still?" I asked.

"I don't think so," Sapia said. "But you'll meet her. You mustn't worry."

"If I find my friend, I don't need to meet her."

Sapia frowned. "To meet our Lady would be to receive blessings you cannot even imagine."

"I'm sure."

"Have you ever received blessings, John?"

I thought of Yeshua stroking me tenderly in the darkness, kissing my mouth and my chin. "I'll feel blessed if I find my friend," I said to Sapia.

We wound our way together through the dusty catacomb, searching. But Yeshua was nowhere to be found. Eventually, we came to a small circular room with a hole in its floor. A guttering torch hung on one wall. "What is this place?" I asked.

"I rarely come down here," Sapia replied. "I don't think I've actually ever seen this room."

I knelt before the hole and peered into its depths. The space was entirely black, as though the shadows had somehow doubled over upon themselves. In the darkness, however, I felt the possibility of a presence, a body I did not need to use my eyes to see.

"Bring me a torch," I said.

Sapia went to the wall and lifted the torch from its sconce. She handed it to me, and I extended the flame down into the hole, illuminating the mossy depths. There at the bottom of the hole, looking scuffed and dirty but still intact, was Yeshua. He stood facing one of the curved walls, staring blankly at the bricks.

Sapia came to stand beside me and peered into the hole.

"You see, John?" she said.

I turned. "Did you know He was here all along?"

She blinked. "How would I have known that?"

"I told you that I was going to wake your sleepers. You became worried. And you took me directly to Him."

"It was only a guess," Sapia said.

"You're a very good guesser then."

"I have no reason to lie to you," she said. "You must believe that."

"I need a rope," I said.

"I don't know if we have a rope."

"You have a moon, Sapia. And you have an entire forest. You can certainly find a rope somewhere in the house."

"Please don't misunderstand. Everything is here for a reason."

"I don't care about the reasons. I only want to get my friend out of this hole. Get me a rope."

"I'll see what I can do," she said and left us.

I lay on my belly, pushing the torch deeper into the hole so I could get a better look at Yeshua. "I'm sorry," I whispered to Him. "I shouldn't have left you. I won't do it again."

Yeshua continued to stare at the curved wall.

"Do you remember when we went walking by the sea late one night?" I said. "Peter and the others were asleep. But you wanted to go walking. You liked to be in the world. And you particularly loved the sea, the scent of it and the feeling of loose pebbles beneath your feet. There was no sea in the city you came from. So we walked together. You found a shell. Do you remember? It was white with a pattern of red. And we spent a long time looking at the pattern because you thought it was beautiful. I'd lived my whole life on those shores and I'd never paid any attention to the shells. Peter would have scoffed at the idea. But I think the shells are beautiful now too. I've seen a pattern like a bird and one like a fish. I meant to tell you that."

Yeshua did not look up at me. Nor did He seem to hear my story. And I worried, in that moment, that the two of us might never be free of the Gray Palace. My specific thought was: *There is some permanence to all this.* Though what precisely I meant by permanence, I was not sure. I only knew the house felt like a thing that did not change. To enter it was to become part of its nature. It was, somehow, not like life at all. In fact, it was the opposite of life. And soon, Yeshua and I would become the opposite of life too.

I forced myself to put such thoughts aside.

The first order of business was to get Yeshua out of the hole. And then I promised myself we would find the way out. I wouldn't allow the house's permanence to overtake us. I would bring us back to our shells and the sea.

Sapia returned, holding a length of rope gingerly as if it was a serpent. "This was in the theater," she said. "I think a previous caretaker might have used it to fly the gods. Jax isn't there anymore. He's likely fled to some deeper region of the house because he knows he'll be punished for lying to you."

I didn't care about the location of Jax or the nature of

his future punishment. I took the rope in silence and tied one end to the sconce that had once held the torch. I'd learned to tie all manner of knots during my days fishing with my father.

After securing the rope, I tossed the length of it over the edge of the hole.

Thankfully, there was enough of it, and the rope coiled near Yeshua's sandaled feet.

I glanced at Sapia. She didn't look like a villain. Instead, she looked as though she was meant to be wandering in some breezy field of wheat, singing the ancient songs of Patmos. But the truth of the matter was that I had no idea what was actually going on inside her head. "I'm going to trust you not to unfasten the rope while I climb down," I said.

"Why would I unfasten the rope?" Sapia asked. "You don't think I mean to harm you, do you?"

"I don't know what to believe."

Sapia shook her head. "I'm really very sorry about all this."

Despite Jax's warnings, I didn't think Sapia lied when she said she thought the house was a safe place to rest. There was something so guileless about her, a characteristic that actually made me feel a kind of sympathetic concern.

"Are you in danger here, Sapia?" I asked. "Are you trapped in some way?"

"Trapped?" she said, as if the idea had never occurred to her. "No, I'm here because I want to be. Our Lady called to us. And we came."

"But if you decided that you wanted to leave, could you?"

"Of course, I could. But I would never want to do such a thing. Our Lady means no harm. No one here means any harm. You must trust in that. Your friend finds himself in this hole because of an unfortunate accident."

Accident or not, it would do no good to argue with Sapia. Even if she wasn't malicious, she was undeniably deluded.

I pulled the rope once more to make sure it would hold, and then I lowered myself into the hole, descending hand over hand. When I reached the bottom of the pit, I put my arms around Yeshua and hugged Him to me. I told Him once more I was sorry for leaving Him. His body remained stiff, unyielding. I examined Him carefully to verify that He hadn't injured Himself in the fall. Then I began to tie the rope around Him in a manner that would be secure.

Before ascending, I noticed that the walls of the pit were not composed of unbroken stone. Alcoves had been dug into the walls, some ten or twelve of them in all. They were each the size of a large bread oven, though much deeper. I wondered if, perhaps, they'd once been used for wine storage. And yet, they seemed too large for that.

I climbed back up the rope to the lip of the hole and found Sapia waiting, still holding the torch.

"Is he injured?" she asked.

"He's not."

"That's excellent. Now you both still have time to rest."

"We aren't going to rest," I said.

"But our Lady wants you to. She wants everyone to rest."

"How old were you when you came to this house, Sapia?"

"Jax and I were young," she said. "Not quite children, but almost so."

This made sense to me. Sapia still seemed like a child, as if she'd stopped maturing the moment she entered the Gray Palace. I realized I was going to have to find a way to get out from under her watchful gaze. She would never be able to accept or even comprehend my arguments for escape. For her, the Lady of the house was everything.

I focused my strength and pulled on the rope, slowly raising Yeshua from the hole.

When He was free and standing before us once more, Sapia looked at the dirt on his tunic and said, "I have an idea, John. Something that will make you both feel better."

"What's that?" I said.

"Clean clothes," she said. "New vestments to be worn for the celebration."

I found I could not look at her. But I also knew I should not argue. I was, at least, beginning to formulate a plan.

†

SAPIA LED US to a kind of workroom, a small circular space adjacent to the atrium. I hadn't glimpsed the room before because its entrance was obscured. A black spider-like loom dominated the room's center, and near the loom's beam sat an old woman in a wooden chair. She reminded me of the sort of matron one might find outside one of the tenement houses of Jerusalem. Her face was fleshy. Her eyes, small and dark. She used the head of a prickly plant to comb a piece of wool folded in her lap. Around her lay piles of gray garments similar to those I'd seen the sleepers wearing.

"Weaver," Sapia said in a tone that made me think the old woman might be a slave, "these good men are in need of raiment for the celebration."

The weaver ceased her combing and looked up from the wool to assess Yeshua and me with her dark eyes. She placed the prickly plant and piece of wool carefully on a table next to her chair and stood with some difficulty. All of the weaver's movements were practiced and slow. It seemed to me that time even moved differently in her presence. With a labored breath, she sorted through one of the several piles of gray tunics. Shaking dust from two of the garments, she walked toward us, arms extended, one tunic in each hand.

I took both tunics and thanked her. The old woman said nothing in return. Instead, she went to a black hook from which hung a series of corded necklaces. At the end of each cord dangled a small hand made of copper, the same sort I'd seen Master Drusus wearing. The hand looked as though it had once gripped something spherical. Each miniature hand was the same shape as the doorknocker at the front of the house.

The weaver took two of the cords and brought them to me.

I accepted the necklaces and said to the weaver, "Do you live here as well?"

The old woman turned away without speaking. She made her way back to her wooden chair, sat down and took up her wool and prickly plant again to resume her brushing.

"The weaver doesn't mean to be rude, John," Sapia said. "She rarely speaks. She's been here a long time. Much longer than Jax and me."

"And what will she do during this so-called celebration?" I asked, hoping to gain more information.

"Well, I suppose she'll stay in this room," Sapia said. "Just as she always does. Our Lady will know what to do with the weaver when the time comes. She knows what to do with everyone." Sapia smiled.

I attempted a smile in return.

†

"THIS IS NOT an experience I would have chosen for us," I told Yeshua as I worked to remove his soiled tunic in our sleeping chamber. Sapia had left us alone with our new gray garments, a plate of food and a basin of water to wash ourselves. It would be better if we, at least, appeared to be following her instructions. Compliance would hopefully allow us to move more freely around the house.

Yeshua stood naked before me, and as I washed Him, I could not help but think of what had once been between the two of us. In the beginning, our intimacy had seemed almost trance-like. As if we both understood that we must not do the acts we did. Yet we were compelled to do them by some force beyond us. Or perhaps, that perception was entirely my own. For it was often difficult to understand how Yeshua felt about what we did when we were alone together. More than anything, it seemed that He wanted a feeling of comfort, of safety. And because of this, He mirrored my own actions. I remembered feeling that our bodies moved almost mechanically when we first began touching. Over the months that followed, these actions became something more intense. Together, we developed a secret language, a set of rituals, that both of us held in highest esteem. When we were alone in the space of our room, we became more than Yeshua and John. We were a creature that did not exist in Galilee. A fine animal that I thought might not exist anywhere else in the world.

Yeshua's body was now not so very different than it once had been. Thinner perhaps, but not as thin as it should have been, considering the fact that He no longer ate. I'd done my best to feed him, believing that if I let Him go hungry, He would die. But Yeshua, in His new state, could not chew. Could not swallow. Still, He did not waste away. For my part, I felt constantly famished. I ate the unleavened bread and honey Sapia had left in our room, knowing I'd likely need the sustenance for what was to come.

Our new tunics fit snuggly, leaving few folds, and I realized there was nowhere to conceal Peter's knife. So instead of tucking the knife in my belt as I'd done before, I cut a long strip from my old tunic and tied the knife to my outer thigh so that it was hidden under the gray fabric. This was not ideal, as it would be difficult to access to the blade. But it was better than abandoning the weapon in our room entirely.

"We're both going for a walk this time," I said to Yeshua after I'd dressed Him.

His black eyes stared somewhere to the left of me.

I went to the door of our room and passed through the curtain.

To my great relief, Yeshua followed.

†

WE MADE OUR way together through the atrium and into the dark woods where the false moon still glowed in its painted sky. Yeshua was left unmoved. And though I knew I shouldn't have expected a reaction from Him, I was still disappointed that even a marvel such as this could not excite His passions. He'd once been so startled by beauty, pausing often to observe commonplaces. Not only the shells on the beach but palm fronds and the ripples of water too. At times, it had seemed as if He was *seeing* for the first time.

From the forest, we entered the amphitheater, which was now unoccupied, just as Sapia had reported. A large wooden door stood at the rear of the stage between two fluted columns. Winged figures, half-man and half-bird, were painted on the pediment above the door. The bird-men leered at us with yellow eyes as we approached. I touched the door's brass handle, hoping it wouldn't prove to be another of the house's illusions. But the handle moved just as any door handle would. Turning it, I experienced feelings of both excitement and dread. For we were about to enter a section of the house that was, as of yet, unfamiliar. It seemed almost as though we were setting out on a voyage to a new country.

I paused long enough to take Yeshua's hand, lacing my fingers through His. Then, grasping the handle once again, I opened the door. Beyond the painted facade of the stage lay something I could not have imagined in such a house as the Gray Palace. We stepped into a room that appeared to be entirely conventional in nature. It was, in fact, the kind of sitting room one might encounter in any noble house. Three wooden chairs were arranged at the room's center in a triangular configuration. On a low lacquered table nearby was the bust of some figure I did not recognize, perhaps a statesman or a senator. And a large lacquered desk stood against the far wall beside a brazier meant for keeping a fire.

The only other detail of note in the sitting room was a small arched window painted onto one wall. Such painted windows were a common enough sight, even in Jerusalem, for it was widely agreed that actual streets, with their filth and teeming crowds, were not pleasant to look upon.

Painted windows traditionally depicted settings of a more inviting nature.

This particular painted window, depicted what appeared to be a walled Roman garden, but it was not the sweet and sunlit space that might have been expected. Instead, the garden bore an undeniable sense of melancholy, like a tomb than a setting for an idyll. A path of loose stone cut through the center of the garden. Roses, marigolds and hyacinth grew on either side of the path. Yet even the colors of the flowers were muted, as if some unpleasant vapor had crept forth and settled over them.

At the back of the painted garden stood a row of misshapen dwarf trees, and beyond the trees, a series of stone alcoves had been cut into the high wall. In one alcove stood a gray shape that I, at first, took to be a statue. Yet something about the figure's posture caused me to want a closer look.

Approaching the painted window, I saw that the shape in the alcove was actually the figure of a tall woman. She was draped in a long gray shawl. And she bowed her head, perhaps in sorrow or in prayer.

I took a step closer still and, from my new perspective, saw that the figure held something in one of her long-fingered hands. The object was small and round. I leaned closer but couldn't make out any qualities of the object, not even its color. I knew only that the object was important to the woman because of the way she clutched it. I also understood, almost immediately, that this figure was meant to be a depiction of Sapia and Jax's mysterious Lady. The hand that clutched the object was the same as the hand I wore on the cord around my neck. It was the model for the brass door knocker as well.

The more I looked at the Lady, the more I began to feel that she was in a state of profound despair. Discontent flowed from her, bleeding outward, coloring the garden. The emotion threatened to color even the room beyond the painting. The room in which I stood.

I backed slowly away from the painted window and returned to Yeshua who had wandered to the far side of the room to stand beside the imposing desk. Various pieces of papyrus lay spread across the desk as if someone had recently been studying them. There were diagrams drawn on the papyrus, none of which I could properly understand. They appeared to depict a large machine, complete with a system of gears and pulleys. Also depicted was a complex network of pipes. Markings seemed to indicate the pipes carried some kind of substance from one place to another, and I wondered if the substance might be water. I'd heard from my uncle that Rome had marvelous methods for moving water from one place to the next.

"Do you make anything of these?" I asked Yeshua.

He, of course, made no response.

"I suppose we should move on then," I said, glancing back at the painted window and the Lady there.

†

WE MADE OUR way through a carved door set in the far wall of the sitting room. As soon as we reached the next room, I stopped, unable to fully comprehend what I saw. For the room beyond the door was *identical* to the previous room, the same three wooden chairs, the same bust of a statesman, the same desk and brazier. Except here, every surface had been painted a startling, nearly-luminescent white, from the stone of the floors to the vaults of the ceiling to each piece of furniture. Even the painted window looking out on the garden had somehow been rendered in varying shades of white. The tall woman who stood in the garden was white as well. And there was some difference in her posture. After studying her more carefully, I realized she was no longer quite so lost in sorrow or prayer. She'd raised her head, ever so slightly. And though I still couldn't see her eyes, it occurred to me that the reason she'd raised her head was to look out at Yeshua and me. This was illogical, of course. The painting in the white room was, in fact, a different painting than the one that had come before. Yet I could not help but feel that the presence in the paintings was the same. The Lady had followed us from one room to the next.

A silence crept over us in the white room, as if color was not the only quality that had been drained from the space. The paint had a muffling thickness about it. I was afraid that, if I were to speak, I would not hear my own words.

Yeshua appeared as though He did not want to linger in this strange white room either. He'd already passed through a door on the far wall, and I followed him. The next room, if it could be called a room at all, was painted entirely black. Once again, all of the furnishings matched those of the original sitting room: three chairs, a bust, and a large desk covered in scraps of papyrus. But this time, some tar or resin had been used to cover everything. A shadow on the wall of the black room indicated the painted garden. And in the garden, once more, stood the female figure, now almost entirely indistinct. What was most unsettling, however, was that I had the sense that she'd raised her head even further. Nearly enough to look out at us.

I felt that to be seen by this figure would be to be changed by her. Even her rooms were enough to change a man. Moving between the three identical spaces made me feel as though none of the rooms, including the initial sitting room, were real. In fact, it made me feel as though nothing in the entire house was quite real. All of it had, in some way, been manipulated.

I thought again of the door at the back of the house, the exit Jax had promised. We had to find the door, and soon.

†

BEHIND THE NEXT door was a room, neither black nor white, but gray. And unlike the rooms that came before, the gray room did not pretend to be a common living space. It was, instead, a circular stone chamber, empty but for a curious mechanism rising from the center of the floor. The mechanism was composed of a large spoked wheel fastened horizontally to a wooden post. A series of grooved lines, applied in groups of two and three, marked the rim of the wheel.

I was reminded of another wheel I'd encountered in my village once: a *Rota Fortuna.* That wheel had belonged to a traveling Greek, and it too was marked with a series of indecipherable symbols. The Greek invited patrons to spin the wheel, and from the resulting position, he told their fortunes. I had no real interest in the Rota Fortuna, as I did not believe in fortune. Such concepts were connected to the antique tales of my mother, the tales that had been wrapped in the dressings of her madness. However, unlike the Rota Fortuna, the wheel in the gray room decidedly drew my interest. For the only other feature of the space was a doorway on the far wall that appeared to be filled in with stone. If there was some way to move beyond the gray room, it likely had something to do with the wheel.

Yeshua walked the perimeter of the circular room, and I examined the wheel, placing my hand on the rim and attempting to turn it. When the wheel wouldn't budge, I put both hands on the rim, applying all of my force. Suddenly, the entire room seemed to shift under my feet. I stumbled back from the wheel, unsure what had just happened. Yeshua too paused. I approached the wheel once more, gripping the rim and applying all of my strength as I moved it. This time, the entire room began turning upon what must have been some unseen axis. The sealed door on the far wall slid across the stone, finally matching with another door that led into a separate space. The room beyond the now open door was a dark void. And rather than exploring the space, I continued to turn the wheel and the gray room rotated further, revealing a variety of other openings. Each, I understood, was a possible outcome. Not unlike the fates of the Rota Fortuna

I stopped at one of the later openings and approached the door. The room beyond appeared to be a dining room with low couches surrounding a large gilt table. Bones of animals littered the floor. There was no exit from the dining room other than the opening created by the wheel. This meant that if someone in the gray room turned the wheel, a person standing inside the dining room would be trapped, sealed off from the rest of the house. I shuddered at the thought of being imprisoned in such a place and knew I would have to be careful about which room I chose to enter.

Spinning the wheel, I caused another space to appear. This one contained what looked like a series of marble sculptures, perhaps the gods themselves, their backs turned toward the door. The shadowy figures reminded me of the gray woman in the painted garden, and I found I did not want to look at them further.

I turned the wheel again. The next room that came into view was no room at all. It appeared, quite impossibly, to be a large body of water—a black lake, shimmering beneath a starlit sky. A murky, stagnant odor wafted toward me from the room. And I saw that the threshold of the doorway met the edge of a stony shore. On that shore was a wooden boat with oars resting in its weathered hull. I glanced at Yeshua. He too stared at the lake. "Should we take the boat?" I said. "There could be a door on the other side."

Yeshua said nothing in return.

I stepped through the door and onto the pebbled beach, the soles of my sandals shifting loose stone. Yeshua, thankfully, followed. And from my new vantage point, I saw that, at the center of the dark lake, was a small wooded island. On the shore of that island was a second boat. Its presence suggested that someone had traveled to the island before us, someone who might still be there and could perhaps provide a clue to finding the exit.

I took Yeshua's cold hand, and He allowed me to guide Him to a bench in the boat's stern. Once He was seated, I pushed off from the shore and jumped into the bow, taking up the oars. I was reminded, in that moment, of the shores of Galilee. How many fishermen's boats had I boarded there? How many times had I been with Peter and the others upon the sea? As we floated on the black lake, I felt a pang of grief. Even the dreadful fishing boats provoked nostalgia. Yeshua and I were now so far away from everything we knew. And somehow far from any imaginable future too.

I rowed across the dark waters of the lake, considering the stars in the nighttime sky. The illusion in this room was so complete. There was no sense of a surrounding house. I did not know how the architect had caused the sky to grow so black or the stars to shine so brightly. I knew only that I felt as though I was on a lake at midnight. In this moment, that was the only imaginable truth.

When we were halfway across the lake, a male figure carrying a lantern appeared on the shore of the distant island. He stood near the second rowboat and peered out at us. "Who's there?" the figure said.

"I am called John," I replied.

"John? And Peter?" the figure said. He brought the lantern closer to his face then. It was the tall fair-haired soldier from that morning who'd told us his partner recognized Yeshua. The very man who'd advised us to find a place in Rome to hide.

"Gallus," I said, more than a little concerned at his presence. For though the soldier had been seemingly kind to us, I had no idea why he would be here inside the Gray Palace. I'd once heard a story of a soldier rescuing a man from a fire in Jerusalem and then beating him to death because the man did not laud the soldier with enough blessings. I wondered if Gallus had come to beat me now too.

As we neared the island, the soldier, dressed in his short tunic, sword belt and dark cloak, waded into the water to grab hold of our boat's prow.

The bloody color of his cloak made me think of Yeshua writhing on the cross, howling beneath a colorless sky.

"Stay back," I called.

The soldier stopped.

"We don't need your help," I said. "We'll do this ourselves."

Gallus remained in the water, watching as I debarked and pulled our vessel to the shore of the island.

Yeshua sat in the stern, so empty and frail. And as I looked at Him, I realized I had never felt quite as alone as I did in that moment. His absence, the desolation of it, spread across the dark waters. I turned, once more, to the soldier. "How did you come to be in this house?" I said, realizing that I sounded much like Regulus, the mad aristocrat who believed he saw words in trees.

Gallus waded back to the shore and lifted his lantern. His face looked hollower than it had that morning and wearier too. "My partner, Magnus, insisted that we search for the two of you. He told me he remembered what had happened to your Peter in Jerusalem." Gallus looked at Yeshua. "And Magnus said His name is not Peter."

A feeling, colder than the waters of the black lake, moved through me. "Where is Magnus now?"

"We were separated." Gallus gazed off into the darkness. "This house is willfully confusing."

"Did he tell you what he remembered?"

Gallus shook his head. "He was distracted. Magnus questioned a number of slaves, and we learned that you and your companion had come here to the Gray Palace."

"Do you know why it's called that?"

"Because it lies upon Rome like a fog," Gallus said. "There are those who believe the house is restorative in its nature. But there are also many rumors of men and women who have gone missing here. We soldiers have been waiting for an edict that will grant us the right to search the Gray Palace. But the mistress of the house seems to have certain influences upon the city."

"Influences?"

"Over the senate," Gallus said. "The men of power."

"Yet you came today without your edict," I said.

"Magnus insisted."

"And how did you get inside?"

"A young man admitted us," Gallus replied. "He wore feathers on his shoulders. He disappeared into the walls of the house before we could question him."

I wondered why Jax had allowed two soldiers to enter the Gray Palace. He'd said no one else was to be admitted. Was he merely trying to cause trouble? Or was there something more to this act?

"I came to the island perhaps an hour ago," Gallus said. "I searched it and—" He hesitated.

"And?"

"I made a troubling discovery."

It occurred to me that the light of the lantern wasn't the only thing that made Gallus look so hollow. Something inside him had changed. And I wondered if this change had anything to do with his discovery.

"What did you find?"

Gallus glanced toward a small grove of trees. "It is difficult to explain. I will show you instead."

I didn't know if we should go with this soldier whose partner seemed to recognize Yeshua for the man that He was. And yet, if Gallus could show me something related to the mystery of the house, such a revelation might help us find the exit. So I agreed to follow him. Yeshua and I went with Gallus into the trees to a spot that might have been at the very center of the island. And there we saw a kind of iron door in the sand.

"The door was partially covered," Gallus said. "I had to dig it out."

"And what's below?"

Gallus gripped the handle of the door. With some effort, he turned it, and the door swung open. Beneath were the wooden rungs of a ladder leading down.

†

GALLUS CLENCHED THE lantern handle between his teeth as we descended. Yeshua remained in the forest above, as there was no way to bring Him down the ladder. Though I'd promised I would not leave His side again, the island was small enough, and I believed He would surely be safe for a short while.

Yellow lamplight spilled over the stony walls of the shaft as we moved deeper into the earth. The air grew dense and damp, and soon the rungs of the ladder became slick with moss. My sandaled foot slipped. I clutched at the rungs.

"Hold fast," Gallus said around a mouthful of his lamp's handle. "It is not much further."

"But where does the ladder lead?" I said.

"You will see," he said. And that was his only reply.

I considered the fact that this entire episode might be a trap set by the two soldiers. Perhaps they wanted to separate Yeshua and me in order to subdue us. But if they intended arrest, a ruse seemed unnecessary. The soldiers had swords after all, and they didn't know I carried Peter's knife. They could have simply taken us by force. It was more likely that Gallus actually intended to show me something, though what it was, I could not imagine.

When we reached the floor of the vault below, the cause of all the dampness became apparent. The vault was flooded. Dark water came up to our knees, perhaps having leaked in from the lake that surrounded the island. Gallus raised his lantern high. The vault's walls were lined with a series of shadowed recesses similar to those dug into the walls of the pit where I'd found Yeshua hours before. But unlike the holes in the wine cellar, *these* holes were not empty. Shapes rested inside. I strained to see what occupied the holes, and my mind, at first, refused to believe what I knew to be true—there were human bodies lying inside the recesses, men and women, the tops of their damp heads protruding.

"Is this some burial vault?" I asked, feeling suddenly even colder than I had a moment before.

"I do not think so," Gallus said. "It is more troubling still. Look here." He brought the lantern close to one of the holes, revealing what appeared to be the desiccated corpse of a woman, cheeks sunken and long white hair matted against her scalp. She was dressed in one of the gray tunics from the weaver's room, and she wore a cord around her neck with an empty hand-shaped medallion hanging from it. Gallus motioned for me to lean closer, and when I did, I saw that the woman's face was not actually desiccated but covered in a fine grayish moss. The moss was similar to the plant matter I'd seen growing on the lips of Master Drusus who'd occupied the room adjacent to our sleeping quarters. This woman, however, bore a great deal more of the moss on her face. A milky lace of spore-like tendrils spilled over the bridge of her nose and down around her thin lips. Small waxy flowers sprouted from foliage on her cheeks. Moss even grew in the seams of the woman's eyelids. Like Master Drusus, she too had the sweet smell of nature about her. It was as if she had become a kind of human garden.

"Is she dead?" I asked, almost hoping that she was.

Gallus gestured toward the woman's chest where her ribcage rose and fell, indicating shallow breaths. "They are all like this." He shone his lamp over the other holes. "I believe they are the missing men and women of Rome. Or some of them at least. But as to what drew them to this place—"

"Yes," I said. "What?"

Gallus shook his head. "I hoped you could help me answer that question."

"Me?"

"You chose to come here, did you not?"

"My friend brought us."

"He is not your brother?" Gallus said.

I realized I'd made a mistake. My story didn't match the story I'd told Gallus and Magnus earlier, that we were brothers and traveling merchants. But in the strange light of the Gray Palace, such details no longer seemed important. "He is not."

"What reason did He give for coming here?" Gallus asked.

"He doesn't give reasons. He's mute."

"Do you not find some way to communicate?"

"I follow Him," I said. "I'm meant to protect Him."

"Is He an important man?"

"Important to me."

Gallus considered this. "You should know that I don't mean you harm. You or your friend who is important to you."

"And yet you came here searching for us."

"It was Magnus who wanted to find you. I am interested in the house for reasons of my own."

"What reasons?"

Instead of answering, Gallus raised his lantern once more, as if looking for some further clue to the meaning of the chamber. The light revealed a series of smaller holes in the wall above. I didn't know what the smaller holes might be for, but they caused me to think of the ropes and pulleys and the narrow pipes I'd seen earlier in the architectural drawings.

"Everything in the house appears abandoned," Gallus said. "All of the rooms, disused. It's as if the Lady has forgotten these places, or perhaps she no longer needs them."

"There's to be a celebration," I said. "Some kind sacrifice."

He raised an eyebrow. "Who told you that?"

"Nearly everyone I've spoken to."

"And what is the sacrifice?"

"I don't think any of them know."

"A ritual in an empty house," Gallus said, "where everyone appears to be in some unconscious state."

I wondered how long this woman had been down here growing moss. How was it possible she'd remained alive? I leaned closer to her, as if she might tell me her secret. A sweet mossy smell rose from her flesh.

"John," Gallus said, "I do not think you should do that."

I realized he was likely correct. As I returned to a standing position, the empty bronze hand that hung on the cord around my neck brushed the top of the woman's head.

Her moss-covered eyelids snapped open. The woman appeared startled at first, as if I'd wakened her from a dream. She craned her neck, peering at me and then at Gallus. Her eyes were glassy. Her pupils, overlarge. She opened her mouth as if to speak. But no words came from her throat. Instead, there was a crackle from deep inside her. Air hissed through the grayish moss that filled her mouth. The hiss intensified as she shifted, attempting to free herself from the hole.

I stumbled backwards, tripping over my own feet and falling into the dark water.

Several of the other figures began shifting in their own chambers, waking from their mysterious sleep. Soon, they too made hissing sounds. The whole space reverberated with the noise.

"What is this?" I said to Gallus.

"It did not happen before. But I also did not make the mistake of touching them."

At that moment, the woman I'd awakened fell from her hole and into the water with a great splash. She struggled to stand.

"Return to the ladder," Gallus said, drawing his sword and stepping between the woman and me. "Go now."

I did as he commanded, not wanting to stay in this place a moment longer.

"Citizen," Gallus said to the moss-covered woman who rose up from the water. "Stay back. I do not wish to harm you."

At the top of the ladder, I found Yeshua waiting. Taking His hand, I guided Him through the forest toward our boat. We'd nearly reached it when I felt Him tug against me. I turned and saw He'd stopped to gaze back at the forest, apparently listening to the hissing sounds that rose from the hole. "Yeshua," I said, "what is it? Now is not the time to—" But then, I grew silent. For Yeshua began to turn back toward me, and I felt that, when I saw His eyes, they would again be the eyes of my beloved. He would have awakened. He would have returned to Himself. Perhaps the bodies in the hole were the reason He'd come to this house in the first place. Yeshua did not like to see suffering. And the suffering of the men and women in the pit appeared to be extraordinary indeed.

But before Yeshua could fully turn, Gallus came crashing through the forest. “Boat! There is danger!”

I looked to the forest behind him.

From between the trees, a single figure emerged, one of the bodies from the pit, a tall man, dressed in the same gray vestments as the woman. Gray moss dangled from his face like an overgrown beard. The male figure moved unnaturally, walking as if his legs were no longer quite connected to his hips. He stumbled after Gallus, making low hissing sounds. His gray mouth hung open. And the expression on his face looked almost like a grin.

Gallus grabbed Yeshua and me by the arms and nearly threw us into the rowboat.

The gray thing intensified its hissing.

Other figures appeared from the forest then, all of them grinning and walking on unsteady legs. Their grins made me think they understood some secret. A terrible truth that gave them pleasure.

Gallus pushed the boat into the lake and hurled himself into its fore. He plunged the oars into the water, putting distance between us and the island.

The gray figures from the pit did not pause at the water’s edge. Instead, they continued to walk, as if they did not see the dark water. They walked until their heads were submerged. And finally they were gone.

“Did they drown themselves?” I asked.

“I do not think so,” Gallus said.

“How do you know?”

"Because I ran one through with my sword and—"

At that moment a pale hand reached up from the water, gripping the edge of our boat.

"Gallus!" I said

The soldier raised an oar and brought it down upon the hand with great force. The hand disappeared. But by then there was another hand on the opposite side of the boat, rocking us. The gray figures were beneath the boat, and I feared they would soon topple us into the black water.

"Keep them back," Gallus said.

He rowed as I worked to pry slippery gray fingers from the hull. Gallus maneuvered us around the tree-covered island, not toward the open door that led back to the gray wheel room, but toward the opposite wall that hovered in the distance like some dark and disused ruin.

"There is another door," Gallus said. "I saw it from the island."

I was so shaken, I could not even formulate a response. Instead, I wondered what the Lady of the house had done to these men and women to transform them. And I wondered too if they could be cured or if such a life was all that remained.

†

THE SECOND DOOR rose before us, a great bronzed plate decorated with scenes from a myth that I vaguely recognized. Perhaps a tale about the making of the world.

A gathering of flowers and birds was carved in bas relief. Wings became petals, and petals became wings. The large door would surely be locked. We would not be permitted to move beyond the lake. We'd be trapped here with the bodies that wanted to pull us down into the water. But after Gallus dragged the boat onto the stony strip of shore, he opened the bronzed door with no difficulty, revealing what appeared to a small cube-shaped room built of wooden boards. A dust-covered lever protruded from one wall.

"We should move quickly," Gallus said, looking out across the water, as if he thought the gray people might rise up at any moment.

"What is this room?" I asked, helping Yeshua from the boat.

"A lifting mechanism, I believe. I have seen one like it on Palatine Hill, used to transport the emperor's lions."

"Lions?"

"Get in," he told me.

I stepped inside the small wooden room with Yeshua in tow. Gallus followed, closing the bronzed door behind us. He pulled the lever mounted on the wall, and the lift shuddered to life. We were drawn rapidly upward via some system of counterweights. My belly clenched. Through cracks between the wooden boards, the black waters of the lake grew distant. Thankfully, there was still no sign of the moss-covered people. When the lift finally shuddered to a halt, Gallus opened the door, and I saw that we were suspended at a great height in the nighttime sky above the island. There was no floor beneath us. Instead, some one hundred glimmering lamps filled the space, each suspended on a finely-wrought chain. The lamps looked like stars.

Before us, meeting the floor of the lift, was another kind of conveyance, a wooden pallet that hung suspended from a pulley system. "Why would anyone create such a complicated thing as this?" I asked.

"The Lady has her reasons," Gallus said. "If we find some firmer ground, I will tell you what I know." The soldier put one foot onto the pallet that was suspended in the air, testing to make sure the platform remained secure. He stepped out onto the pallet and turned to offer his hand. He helped me onto the platform, and I, in turn, helped Yeshua. There was part of me that believed, when I touched Yeshua, He might pause again as he had on the island. But He did not. He remained an empty chalice. And I wondered if He would ever be full again.

†

THE WIRES AND pulleys supporting the pallet formed a complex system of tracks that crisscrossed the false sky. Gallus navigated the tracks as if sailing a ship, and we travelled between patterns in the stars. Some of the patterns were familiar constellations: the hunter, the cup, the altar. My mother had murmured such names in the darkness of her room. She said the stars had risen out of the firmament, unchanging. Yet, here in the Gray Palace, it appeared that certain constellations had been omitted or altered. Where, for instance, were the ram and the greater dog? And what was the curious shape in the distance that looked like a laurel flower blooming?

"The stars," I said. "They're different."

"Because she owns them," Gallus said. "The Lady does as she pleases. As with everything else in this house."

We came to a black wooden bridge suspended in the sky, and the three of us left the pallet to cross it.

"Are you searching for the exit?" I asked.

"I am not."

"What then?"

"I am looking for the Lady herself," the soldier replied. "I have questions for her."

†

YESHUA AND I followed Gallus across the bridge to a door that appeared to hang suspended amongst the stars. In truth, its frame was mounted on a black and painted wall. Like so much else in the Gray Palace, this levitation proved nothing more than mere illusion. The door opened onto a room, bone-white like a sepulture and lit with carved ivory torches. Occupying nearly the entire space of the floor was an astonishingly elaborate model made of baked clay. The model depicted a city, vast in its proportions, built on a series of low-lying hills and containing everything from pillared temples to a wide and painted river to the narrows of a crooked slum. Every street and fountain, every house and alley was so precisely rendered as to make me feel I should be able to walk the empty boulevards.

"Rome," Gallus said, circling the model. "She has all of it here." He pointed to a low-lying building with the appearance of a horse's stable. "This is the house where I once lived. And there," he said, pointing to a more substantial structure, "that is the hall where I took my soldier's training."

Yeshua paid no attention to the miniature city. Instead, He moved to one corner of the room and stared absently at the pale wall.

"But what could be the purpose of this model?" I asked. "Is it another puzzle?"

Gallus crouched to inspect the model more closely. "I do not believe anything in this house is meant to be solved."

"What then?"

The soldier ran his finger delicately along the grooved rooftop of a temple on a hill. "Roman men have always fled to strange gods," he said. "And I think the Gray Palace may very well be the strangest god of them all." He lifted his hand from the temple and inspected the fine layer of white dust on his fingertip. "I do not know how such things are where you come from, John, but here, the common deities of the state are seen as little more than hollow idols. The men and women of this city have sought to drink from a deeper well since the she-wolf suckled the boy twins in the age of bronze. I, for one, have witnessed every sort of desperate worship here—orgiastic processions and wild dancing and primitive blood-lettings. All of it, such a frantic search. The Gray Palace, however, promises something beyond another Roman cult. It goes beyond mere ritual. Perhaps even beyond that which is human."

"What do you mean?"

"I have made a study of this place," Gallus said. "And I have a theory about its nature."

"What drew you to study the Gray Palace?"

"It is a difficult story," the soldier said. "And I am not one to speak so many words. But I will tell you as best I can." He appeared to steel himself as if in anticipation of a blow. "I too had a friend I followed, you see. A man who was good and kind, called Antonius Pontifex. A revered soldier of the High Pretorian Guard."

I did not imagine that a soldier of the High Pretorian Guard could be either good or kind. But the pained expression on Gallus's face prevented me from saying as much.

"Before I tell you what I know of the house, you should understand something of my own history," Gallus said. "I was captured some years ago in the great forests of the North, taken from my tribe and my family and brought here as a slave. The Romans put me to work in the stone quarries at the city's southern edge. They nearly broke my back, forcing me to lift wide flat stones and place them in wheeled carts. The masters whipped me when I did not move quickly enough. At times, they whipped me for their own pleasure too. My size and strength became a kind of spectacle, a living symbol of the empire's dominance. For if Rome could subdue a giant such as me, clearly they could subdue anything at all."

"Rome is cruel," I said, glancing at Yeshua. "I know that well enough."

Gallus lowered his head. "They mocked me as I worked, calling me the Great Prince of the North. And it is, perhaps, because of that name that Pontifex first heard of me. He was not like other soldiers. He was gentle. Sometimes he even spoke with humor. He brought bread and wine to the slave house. He talked with me at length, asking questions about the forests of my youth and the people who lived there. He asked if I knew of the great burning man and of the mistletoe cut from trees with golden sickles. Pontifex held secrets within him. I could tell as much when I looked into his eyes. And each time I talked to him, I found I wanted to know more.

"Eventually, Pontifex took me away from the slave house and kept me in his own home. He fed me and tended to my wounds. He taught me to better speak his language. Soon, he allowed me to sleep alongside him in his bed." Gallus grew still. The weight of some vast emotion seemed to fill the room. "I had been treated like a dog for such a long time," he continued. "But Pontifex made me feel, once more, like a man. Over the months that followed, I found myself forgetting the North, the black oceans there, the forests of Oak and Ash. I realized I would not return to that place even if the empire set me free. I wanted to be at this man's side. We had become something more together.

We were—" Gallus searched for the right words.

"As one?" I said.

The soldier looked relieved I had spoken the words first. "As one, yes. And, as we grew closer, I came to understand something of why he had first shown an interest me. Pontifex had concerns beyond mere armories and battle."

"What concerns?"

"Matters of what he called the 'invisible world,'" Gallus said. "His father had been a priest in the underground temple of Mithras, a religion brought here from the East. As a youth, Pontifex acted as a kind of agent to his father. Together, they sought to better understand the soul and its dominions. They became investigators of the supernal plane, looking to discover that which lay just beyond the tangible scrim of our ordinary existence. When his father died, Pontifex took the mantle of this search entirely upon himself."

"And what did you have to offer him in terms of these investigations?" I asked.

"He wished to learn about the priests of North," Gallus said, "the so-called Druids observed by Julius Cesar in his travels. He thought I might be the man to teach him. In those days, he was already trying to gain access to this house, the Gray Palace. He had reason to believe that the mistress of the house had come from the North. There was conjecture that she was a Druid priestess, brought to Rome by Cesar himself some years ago to act as his concubine."

"And?" I said, "was she that?"

Gallus shook his head. "The Lady is no Druid. Pontifex let go of that idea soon enough. But he maintained his interest in me. He said he sensed within me the deep vibrations of the forests and the dark surging of the oceans too. He helped me gain status as one of the Cohorts Vigilum, the Firemen of Rome. And from there I became a soldier of the lower echelon, assisting him in his investigations."

"The Gray Place was already the center of a number of unnatural happenings. A group of magi from Arabia were murdered one night at the base of its southern wall. A well-known witch called Indrid claimed the palace concealed an entrance to the underworld. And, as if to confirm this rumor, a dead man was seen entering and exiting the house one evening. There were those of the aristocracy who continued to maintain the house had restorative powers, and all the while, many of those same men and women continued to disappear without a trace.

"The closer Pontifex's investigations came to the Gray Palace itself, however, the more the house seemed to grow quiet, to intentionally recede into its own mists. Pontifex believed this to be a bad omen. He thought the Gray Palace was in the process of gathering some energy, preparing to lash out, possibly at Rome itself."

"And the Lady?" I asked. "Did he discover anything more about her?"

"We raised and dismissed many theories," Gallus said. "For a time, Pontifex believed the Lady was a powerful member of the Julii who had become preoccupied with witchcraft in her youth. Then, he thought she was an Egyptian priestess of Isis who had brought her foreign ways to Rome. And finally that she was some disciple of the Christos who—"

"What?" I said.

"Christos," Gallus repeated, "of the Greek cult. Messenger of the Sun. But the mistress of the Gray Palace is a disciple of no one. The more information we uncovered, the more she appeared to be nothing at all. In fact, that is how Pontifex began to refer to her: The 'Great I Am Not.' She seemed a woman with no qualities. Entirely in absence. And yet, she was also, quite possibly, a representation of all that Pontifex's father had searched for, a purveyor of the invisible world. Pontifex became determined to learn her secrets. He wanted to force the Gray Lady to present herself. He thought perhaps her knowledge could be used for good."

"You always speak of your friend in the past," I said.

Gallus took a breath. "I was called away. My phalanx traveled to the East, to protect the edges of the empire. And it was then that Pontifex attempted to gain entrance to the Gray Palace. He wrote to me in a letter, saying this was the only way to learn the truth. I wrote a response, of course, asking him not to go without me. I said I wanted to remain always at his side. We would make discoveries together. We would fight if need be. And yet—"

"Pontifex would not listen," I said, looking toward Yeshua.

"He was murdered," Gallus said. "Attacked in the street near the Gray Palace by a robber. His throat was slit. He was left to bleed. The only man who ever—" Gallus broke off.

"I'm sorry," I said. I wanted to put my hand on his shoulder, but to touch his Roman armor seemed, if not abhorrent, at least impossible. And so I did nothing. "Do you think what happened to Pontifex had something to do with her?"

"After you study the Gray Lady long enough," Gallus said. "You begin to believe everything has to do with her."

He circled the model of Rome until he stood over what appeared to be a replica of the Gray Palace itself. I recognized the narrow street where I'd waited by the door as well as the wide terrazzo of the meat market. The soldier reached down and took hold of the little house, breaking it from the model with some force. The house was a long rectangular box with what appeared to be several floors that formed a kind of stairstep structure.

"Pontifex used to remind me that, no matter how impenetrable these mysteries appeared, the house was still very much a house. There were a set number of rooms. There were specific things a house could and could not do. He said the Gray Lady was inside somewhere, laying her plans. And it was up to the two of us, Pontifex and Gallus, to discover these plans. But, of course, now there is only me."

I wondered, for a moment, if this was why Yeshua had brought us to this house as well. Perhaps Yeshua and

Pontifex both understood something similar about the so-called Gray Lady.

"How will we find her?" I asked.

"We will work our way through her chambers," Gallus said. "Hall by hall and room by room. She is here. This is only a house. And she is only a woman. One who likely intends nefarious deeds."

"Only a house," I repeated. "And only a woman."

Gallus twisted the model of the Gray Palace, causing the clay to crumble between his fingers and fall to the floor.

It was then that we heard faint music.

†

GALLUS PARTED THE folds of a white curtain at the rear of the model room, and there, sitting in the low-slung chairs of what appeared to be a formal music conservatory were Sapia and her brother Jax. The twins, now dressed in matching gray tunics, made for a curious tableau. Sapia plucked a large stringed instrument that rested across her lap. And Jax held a reed flute to his pursed lips, forming airy notes. Their music sounded like springtime, light and lilting. Yet, at times, there was a note of autumn too. The passing on of life. When the twins realized they were no longer alone, they stopped their playing and looked up at us, eyes bright in the torchlight.

"John," Sapia said, smiling kindly. "And Peter."

"And the handsome soldier too," Jax said.

"Is everything all right?" Sapia asked. "You look a little tired, John."

I did not know how to respond as I found it difficult to believe she would choose so slight a phrase to describe my condition. "I'm not *tired*. I'm exhausted and frightened."

"Frightened?" She appeared surprised. "Of what?"

"You act as though you have no idea what's happening in your own house," I said.

"My sister is merely trying to be polite," Jax said. "That's her nature."

I turned to him. "What place is there for politeness in this house? There are horrors here."

"What does he mean by 'horrors?'" Sapia asked Jax.

"We don't have any horrors," he replied, waving his hand as if to dismiss the thought. "Though I suppose the place might be a bit more interesting if we did."

"What do you call the men and women buried in the pit on the island?" I said.

"Do you mean the sleepers?" Sapia asked. "You haven't disturbed them, have you, John? It's vital not to disturb the sleepers."

"They *attacked* us," I said. "They attempted to overturn our boat."

Sapia looked at Jax, distraught.

"Are you telling us you woke the sleepers?" Jax said.

Gallus stepped forward. "They woke themselves. And we are not here to tell you anything. We have come to speak directly to the Lady of the house."

"Be careful about making demands here, soldier," Jax replied. "Remember you are no longer in the streets of Rome."

"Our Lady will know what to do with the sleepers if they have awakened, won't she Jax?" Sapia said.

"I'm sure she will," he replied.

"Why don't the three of you just sit with us?" Sapia said, gesturing toward several empty chairs. "We'll play some of our music for you. Our Lady will make an appearance once—"

"We need to speak to her now, Sapia," I said. "What she's doing here is...it's dangerous."

"Oh, John, if you only understood," she said. "This is all quite the opposite of dangerous."

"Tell us where she is."

Jax placed his flute on a small table beside his chair and took his sister's hand. "They are determined, aren't they, my dear?"

"Please," Sapia said to us. "Do sit. I'm sure she'll come to us soon."

"John," Gallus said from behind me.

I turned and saw an expression of fresh understanding on the soldier's face.

"What is it?" I said.

"I don't think these two will be able to tell us where she is."

"What do you mean?"

"I believe they know far less than they pretend."

I waited for Sapia and Jax to protest, but they did not.

"Is that right?" I asked them.

Sapia attempted one of her warm smiles. "The workings of the house aren't always for us to understand. Our Lady will come when she deems it's time. All will be made clear."

"When she deems it is time?" Gallus said.

"That's right." Sapia nodded. "She'll manifest."

"Sapia," Jax said in a warning tone.

"What do you mean 'manifest?'" Gallus asked. "Has she not done so before?"

"Of course, she has," Sapia said. "She's manifested in all manner of ways."

"But have you actually seen her? Have you spoken with her?"

The twins fell silent. Then Sapia said, "Our Lady provides messages of every sort. And it is through these messages that we know what we're meant to do."

"How does she provide these messages?" Gallus asked.

"A palm frond in the reflecting pool," Sapia said. "An open door in the atrium. Jax interprets the messages for us."

I looked at Jax. His expression had turned sullen, like a child caught in the act of misbehaving.

"But you have never seen her," Gallus said. "And you have never spoken to her."

"Not directly," Sapia said.

"Then how do you know she actually exists?" I asked

"John," Jax said. "You're going to frighten my sister."

I stared at him in disbelief. "You have scores of men and women imprisoned in this house. Suffering from what appears to be some kind of poisoning. And all you're worried about is me frightening your *sister*?"

"How do you know what to do with the men and women who come here?" Gallus asked. "Your so-called sleepers."

"We don't do anything with them," Sapia replied. "They arrive. They ask for a room. And we allow them to rest."

"In a dark pit at the bottom of a lake?" I said.

"They went to the island of their own accord," Jax said. "Everything they've done is of their own accord. Our Lady speaks to them privately, I suppose. Just as she speaks to us."

"I hadn't considered the fact that all of this might be some kind of self-perpetuating fantasy," Gallus said. "Similar to what certain men are said to experience at oracles."

"You yourself told me that Pontifex had learned specific information about the Lady," I said.

"Mere rumors," Gallus said. "Pontifex documented all manner of stories from the patricians. But none of it could be verified."

"Pontifex?" Jax said, turning toward his sister. "I remember someone with that name. A soldier. We turned him away, didn't we, Sapia?"

"I believe that's right," she replied. "As our Lady wished."

"Yes, he came to the house very late one night," Jax said.

"Far too late for any reasonable person to be outside."

"I think he was drunk," Jax said.

"So you believe it is possible," I said to at Gallus, "that

there is no Lady? That all of this has occurred because of lies and confusion?"

"Lies?" Sapia said.

Jax took her hand once more. "There are no lies here, sister. And no confusion either. You must trust in that, dear."

An idea appeared to come to Sapia. "Jax *has* seen our Lady. In his dream on Patmos. Isn't that right, Jax?"

"That's right," Jax said.

"Our mother died, you see, and our father abandoned us," Sapia said. "I was overcome with grief. Our mother was so beautiful and so kind. For death to take her...the very thought of her buried in the earth was so cruel, so utterly impossible. Then Jax awoke one morning and told me he'd had a dream. A woman, a vision, had spoken to him. She was beautiful and kind, not unlike Mother. She'd summoned us to come to Rome. We traveled here and found the house just as the dream foretold. And Jax knew the work we were meant to do."

"Have you considered your brother may have invented this dream?" I said. "To help you in your grief. That he found this house on accident or by some other means?"

Sapia looked as if I'd struck her. She turned to her brother. "Tell them," she said. "Tell the about your dream."

"I think you're both being absolutely cruel," Jax said to Gallus and me.

"Tell us," Gallus said from behind me. "Explain the dream that drew you here to Rome."

"I'd never tell anyone except Sapia," he said.

"Why not?" Gallus said.

"Because our Lady asked me not to," Jax said.

"In the dream?" Gallus said.

"That's right."

"Listen to me," Gallus said. "It is clear that something is wrong in this house. Men and women come here to get well, to rest. But instead, they grow sick. The rooms are composed of the remnants of some sort of disused and forgotten simulacra. It seems entirely possible that you and Sapia are actually in control here. That there is no Lady."

Jax looked at us coldly. "You're mistaken, soldier."

"How am I mistaken?" Gallus asked.

"Because I have proof she exists."

"Name your proof," Gallus said.

"I heard the Lady singing, just this morning."

"Oh, that's right!" Sapia said. "Jax said the song was beautiful. And we decided to play our instruments for her. So she might hear something beautiful too."

"Where?" Gallus said. "Where did you hear this singing?"

"From deeper inside the house," Jax said.

"How do we get there?" I asked.

"You don't," Jax said.

"What do you mean?"

"There's a part of the house even the caretakers don't have access to. That's where our Lady lives. That's where she's always lived." He looked at Gallus, considering. "I'll show you," he said, standing from his chair. "Follow me."

Gallus, Yeshua and I followed Jax to an open door at the back of the music room.

"Look for yourselves," Jax said, gesturing toward the room. Gallus, Yeshua and I walked inside. The room was an empty space made of pumice, quite unlike any of the rooms that had come before. There was no pretense of simulation here, no mechanism that might reveal some hidden passage. The room appeared, in fact, to have no purpose whatsoever, as if the architect had run out of ideas, and this was an ending of sorts.

"There's no way forward," Gallus said, sliding his fingers along the wall, perhaps searching for a hidden spring. "Where did the singing come from, Jax?"

But as Gallus spoke, I heard the door to the empty room close behind us. Then there was the sound of a lock being thrown.

Gallus lunged at the door and pounded his hand against it. "Let us out."

"You've interfered enough," Jax called.

"We are attempting to understand what is happening in this house," Gallus said.

"Jax," Sapia's voice could be heard from outside the stone room. "You can't simply leave them in there."

"I don't intend to leave them forever, sister," Jax said, "Only until our Lady has completed her celebration."

Gallus banged on the door again. "In the name of Rome, release us."

"Neither you nor the empire has any authority here,"

Jax said. "You must understand that well enough by now."

And with that, we heard the twins' footsteps receding.

†

"What do we do?" I asked Gallus.

He was in the process of further examining the walls of the stone room, running fingers over smooth surfaces, searching for a seam. Yeshua, for his part, stood silently in a corner.

"If Jax is telling the truth," Gallus said, "and he did, in fact, hear a voice coming from beyond this barrier, then there is likely some way through."

"How do we know Jax was telling the truth though?"

"We do not. But, right now, his words are all we have." The soldier walked around the pumice room, still searching, and I thought about how Yeshua's own story was not unlike the story of the house. There'd been a great effort by the others—Thomas, Phillip, Bartholomew and all the rest—to discern His purpose, to know why He'd come out of the desert. But it wasn't until we all let go of such efforts that we finally began to understand.

"You told me the house isn't a puzzle, Gallus," I said.

The soldier turned. The concerned look on his face made him look stronger and all the more handsome.

"You told me the rooms are meant to be experienced, not solved," I said.

"Pontifex likened the Gray Palace to the Greek caves

at Eleusis," Gallus said. "Boys of the village pass through a series of dark chambers where priests and other holy men are dressed as monsters. There are bright lights and terrible sounds. And because of their frightening experience in those caves, the boys are said to be transformed, as the heroes of old were once transformed by their own harrowing adventures. The boys are made into men."

"And so," I said, "if what Pontifex said is true, isn't it possible the house will show us the way, even if we do nothing?"

"I do not know the answer to that question, John."

"Perhaps we should sit," I said. "Perhaps we should try doing nothing for a time."

"I am not accustomed to doing nothing."

"Still, you look as though you might benefit from rest."

Gallus exhaled. "Very well. We will rest for a short while. But only a short while." He unbuckled his sword belt and eased himself into a sitting position, resting his back against the wall. I sat opposite the soldier, and Yeshua stood in one corner of the room, staring blankly.

After a period of silence, Gallus said, "Why does your friend not talk?"

"What?"

"You claim he is mute. But it seems to me something more than that."

A conversation such as this was not what I meant when I said we should do nothing. "He is not the man He once was," I said, hoping to end the discussion there.

"So something happened to Him?"

"I'm afraid so."

"And does that event have anything to do with what Magnus remembered?" Gallus asked. "The occurrence in the east?"

"I don't want to talk about that."

"But you told me your friend led you here to the Gray Palace. Maybe there is something to that fact, John. Something that should be further explored."

I considered the soldier, the sheer presence of his will. And I wondered what would happen if I told him my story. What would happen if I explained everything to Gallus? "If I tell you," I said, "do you promise not to harm Him?"

"You have my word," Gallus replied.

"I'm not sure I know where to begin."

"At the beginning."

"But there might not be a beginning."

"Make an attempt, John."

And so, seated on the floor of the empty room across from the Roman soldier, I spoke all that I remembered.

†

HE CAME TO us from the desert, I told Gallus. Or, at least, that's what we believed. We were a group of young fishermen, living with our families in the small village of Bethsaida at the Northern edge of the Galilean Sea. At evening time, when our nets were folded and our fish were laid on smoking racks, we rested on the darkening shore in a circle of our fathers' wooden boats. We talked to one another of the day. There were seven of us in all. Eight if Judas joined, which became increasingly unlikely due to his disdain for certain members of our group. Peter spoke most frequently. But it was Matthew who saw the Stranger first. Matthew had only one eye due to an accident in childhood, and this deficiency made him more perceptive than most.

"Who is that near the water's edge?" Matthew said, raising a finger to point toward the shore.

We looked into the twilight and saw a man wrapped in a coarse blanket that might have been stolen from a mule. He was tall and lean and covered in dust. And He stood with His feet in the water, knees bent, appearing to be on the verge of collapse.

"It's just my cousin," Phillip said. "Drunk on wine again."

"It isn't your cousin," Matthew said. "Look at Him."

We looked once more. The Stranger swayed precariously.

Peter stood. And when he did, the rest of us stood as well.

"I don't recognize this man," Peter said. He walked toward the Stranger, and we followed. By the time we arrived at the edge of the sea, the Stranger had fallen face first into the water. "Grab him," Peter yelled. "Pull Him out or He'll drown."

We took the Stranger by the arms and legs and dragged Him from the water, turning Him on his back so He could breathe.

The Stranger gasped and coughed.

He was alive.

On Peter's order, we carried Him to one of the boats and propped His body against its hull. I fetched Him a cup of fresh water from the village well. But the Stranger would not drink or even open His eyes. I poured water onto His lips, hoping the coolness of it might revive Him.

The Stranger was too weak to talk. Too weak to even raise His head.

We all sat looking at Him, waiting.

It's difficult to describe how His face appeared that evening. It seems to me that the face was different than the face I came to later know. Simpler somehow. A mere rudiment. The Stranger had black eyes, something like the shining eyes of a fish. And He had a small mouth. A kind of lipless slit. There seemed to be few other features. I don't remember if he had a nose or ears. Perhaps His featureless appearance was caused by the fact that His face was caked in dust. Perhaps the majority of His face was merely obscured.

"Where do you come from?" Peter asked the Stranger. Peter always asked the questions.

The rest of us leaned forward, hoping the Stranger would answer. But His head merely rolled against the hull of the ship. And He stared up at the sky where stars were just beginning to emerge.

"He's mute," Judas said.

The rest of us looked at Judas and wondered if his

words were true. Judas was decidedly not like the rest of us, and because of that, we rarely trusted him. He had bright red hair. And he was the only one of us who did not have a family in Bethsaida. It was said that Judas had come from an island called Kerioth. There were rumors he'd been some kind of prince there. But Judas, for unknown reasons, had been forsaken. Now he was forced to live as a lowly fisherman. Because of his royal lineage, he did not appreciate being commanded by Peter. A prince, after all, took orders from no one.

"He can speak," Peter said. "I heard him making sounds when he coughed up the water."

"Perhaps he speaks a language other than our own," Thomas offered. Thomas was adept at speculation. He made up stories about all manner of things.

Peter thought about this for a moment and drew close to the Stranger. "Is that it?" Peter asked. "Do you come from somewhere far away?"

The Stranger looked at Peter, blinking his dark, fish-like eyes. Then He looked at the rest of us in turn. Finally, He gestured weakly toward the desert.

"You came out of the desert," Peter said. "But where before that? Hazor? Nazareth?"

The Stranger gazed at Peter dumbly.

"I think He's injured," Matthew said. "Like Thomas's stricken uncle."

Thomas nodded. "My uncle couldn't talk for a time. And even after he began to speak, he couldn't remember anything for days."

"What happened to your uncle to cause this?" Peter said.

"He fell and hit his head on a rock," Thomas said. "At least I think it was a rock. He still doesn't remember."

Peter turned back to the Stranger. "Is that it? Did you hit your head on a rock in the desert?"

The Stranger said nothing.

"Let me look at you," Peter said. "I'll tell you if you hit your head."

"How will you know?" Judas asked.

Peter glared at him. "Because there will be a wound."

"There is not always a wound," Judas replied.

"What do you know of such things, Kerioth?" Peter said.

"What do *you* know?" Judas replied.

Peter shook his head in disgust. He stood and went to the Stranger. He put his hands on the Stranger's head and examined His skull, carefully parting the Stranger's lank brown hair, as if he was searching for lice. The Stranger allowed Peter to touch Him. There was something so soft about the Stranger's presence, so utterly permissive. He did not seem like a man who'd spent time in the harsh environs of the desert.

"There is no injury," Peter announced.

"Well," Judas said, "there we have it."

Peter moved back to his place in the circle, facing the Stranger once more. "What's the last thing you remember from before the desert?" Peter asked. "Do you remember your mother or your father?"

The Stranger blinked his black, fish-like eyes. He reached for the cup of water I held.

Peter gestured for me to give Him more water.

"Take only a few sips," Peter said to the Stranger. "If you drink too fast, you'll make yourself sick."

I knelt beside the Stranger and put the leather cup to His dry lips. He took two careful sips of the water, just as Peter instructed. Then He leaned His head back against the hull of the ship and looked into my eyes.

The Stranger's own eyes were not so odd from close proximity. There was, in fact, a beauty in their darkness, and I could see myself reflected in them, as if the eyes were two pieces of polished stone.

"The last thing you remember before you found yourself in the desert," Peter prompted once more. "Tell us."

"Sun," the Stranger whispered.

"The sun?" Peter said.

"Imagine," Judas said. "A sun in the desert."

"Sun," the Stranger said again.

"That isn't a memory," Peter said. "It's just a word. Do you know your name, at least?"

The Stranger reached for the cup of water. Peter gestured for me to give Him more. The Stranger drank from the cup and said "Sun" again.

"He might be mad," Matthew said. "Like John's mother."

I stiffened. "Don't speak of my mother."

Peter glared at Matthew and me and then looked back at the Stranger. "Is there anything else? Anything at all beside the sun?"

"City," the Stranger said.

"A city?" Peter said. "You come from a city beyond the desert?"

The Stranger stared at the water cup.

"Don't give Him more water yet, John," Peter said.

"But He's thirsty," I said.

"Are you a prophet?" Peter said to the Stranger, ignoring what I'd said. "I've heard that prophets live in the desert."

"Madmen live in the desert too," Judas said. "I think Matthew might be right. This man is like John's mother."

"Quiet," Peter said to Judas. He turned back to look at the Stranger. "Do you remember anything else about this city that you come from? Tell us and we'll give you as much water as you can drink."

The Stranger looked at Peter for a long while. Finally, he said, "My father lives there...in a great city...I lived there too for a time."

And then He closed His black eyes and spoke no more to us that night.

†

"BUT HE DID speak more eventually?" Gallus asked in the empty prison-like room of the Gray Palace.

I nodded. "A great deal more." I wanted to tell the soldier all that had transpired, even the parts of the story I'd believed I would never speak out loud. Why I wanted this, I could not say. I felt some growing affinity towards Gallus, to be sure. He was similar to me, alone in a country that was not his own. And he'd lost his beloved too. I'd appreciated his story of Pontifex. I'd admired his passion. Gallus, with his strength and his armor, seemed a kind of organized system. And part of me believed that, if I relayed my own murky narrative to him, the story itself might become more organized. Somehow less ambiguous. Gallus would act as a machine that purified.

So, I spoke, attempting to explain events that I knew could never truly be explained. And Gallus listened, his fine manly face looking ever more intrigued.

"We kept the Stranger in a stable," I said. "The stable belonged to Thomas's father. We gave Him food and water there. And soon, His strength returned. The Stranger was thankful. And, in the weeks that followed, He spoke to us with increasing frequency."

"What did He tell you?" Gallus asked.

"Well, that is the first of the difficulties," I said. "For what He told us proved hard to remember."

"I do not understand."

"His words," I said, "they were not like words as we knew them. They were more like something light and fine that fell down upon us. When His words covered us, they gave us certain pleasures. They made us feel bold, greater than the lowly fishermen that we were. But then His words slipped away. They disappeared, as water disappears into the fissures of the earth after a heavy rain. No matter how much we tried to hold onto the words, they would always slip through our fingers, slip away from our memories. We knew He said something about a city beyond the desert. Something about a father there. The Stranger had lived in the city with His father. And He had playmates in the city, beings that were not like us. Not like men, I mean. We couldn't recall any more than that. We often talked amongst ourselves, trying to piece together fragments of the stories, trying to better understand the Stranger's words. But all of it remained a mystery. Soon, Peter began to act as a kind of interpreter for the Stranger. He claimed to know that the Stranger was an important man. And it was then that he gave the Stranger a name: 'Yeshua,' Peter called Him. Meaning 'to save,' or 'to deliver.'"

"Did the Stranger not give Himself a name as well?" Gallus asked.

I shook my head. "When we asked Him who He was, He would only tell us another story that we could not remember."

"And what did the Stranger have to say about Peter's words, these interpretations?" Gallus said.

"The Stranger, for the most part, said nothing," I replied. "He seemed almost to exist on some other plain. As if there had been some mistake, and He should never have come out of the desert. He'd gotten lost somehow, become separated from his father and from the playmates of his youth. Yet, at the same time, the Stranger appeared to trust Peter. In truth, I don't know if even Peter believed his own stories. He only knew that they *needed* to be true."

"For what reason?"

"Peter has many reasons. But he rarely made them apparent to us. He hates Rome. He hates the prefects and the soldiers. He wants them driven from Judea."

Gallus contemplated this.

"The Stranger continued to speak to us in the days that followed," I said. "And we disciples—for that is what we began to call ourselves—loved Him for His words. Sometimes, the words even made us feel as though we had visited the great city where the Stranger had once lived with His father. We couldn't recall any precise moment from the stories, any detail, but there was an overall impression they left upon us. Peter began to call the Stranger's words Manna."

"The bread that falls from the heavens," Gallus said. "Pontifex spoke of it."

"Holy bread," I replied. "Nourishment from above. Peter would say, 'Let us take some Manna now.' And he would lead Yeshua up to the mount in the grove of olives. Yeshua would speak and the Manna would drift down upon us once more. It surrounded us and became our sustenance. The Manna left us as soon as the Stranger stopped speaking, but—"

"But?"

"It didn't matter to us that we'd forgotten His words. For we believed then that we would never be forced to live in lack again. The Stranger was among us after all. And

He would continue to speak, to give us His Manna. Often when He spoke, we felt as if we had not only eaten the holy bread but also drunk strong wine. We were no longer tethered to the problems of the world. All of us longed for the feeling the Stranger could bring. We looked forward to His words night after night. Other fishermen and farmers began to hear about what Yeshua could do. They too wanted to experience the Manna. Peter began taking Him to groves in other villages. Yeshua stood on mounts and spoke. Soon crowds began to form. Men and women from all over Galilee."

"This is a curious tale."

"I don't think there has ever been one more curious," I said. "Peter used these nighttime meetings to draw himself up to a state of even greater influence. He would always speak after Yeshua spoke, telling us about the Romans, telling us what he had learned from the warlike men in the caves at Qumran. He would tell us that the prefects and soldiers must be driven from our land. And we would listen, still drunk from Yeshua's words. Soon the small villages were not enough for Peter. He took us on a pilgrimage to Jerusalem. He wanted everyone to hear Yeshua's message. And it was in Jerusalem that things began to come apart. There were too many listeners. Too many eyes and ears. And Judas was seduced by the fineries of the Romans. Their luxuries reminded him of what he had lost, his royal days on the island of Kerioth. Peter continued to push his own concerns. And Judas supplied information to the

Romans. Yeshua, for His part, began to feel confused. The only place He'd ever felt truly safe was with—"

"With you," Gallus said.

"Maybe it was because I gave Him water on that first day. Or maybe it was because I so often spoke to Him. I did not treat Him like a stranger. He made it clear that He wanted to stay with me. He wanted me to care for Him. I was to remain always at His side. And night after night we—" Memories flooded the darkened chambers of my mind. Yeshua kissing me on the mouth. Yeshua inside me. Yeshua whispering to me in the dark: *John, I will tell you things I cannot tell the others.* "Events in Jerusalem rose to a great swell, a wave that would crush us. Yeshua was perceived as a danger to the city. The leaders of the temple called Him a devil. He was said to be one of the ancient beasts that crawled forth from the earth, dressed in the skin of a man. His presence caused disorder. Judas told the soldiers where to find Him one night. Yeshua was imprisoned and finally killed. Executed by the Romans."

Gallus looked at Yeshua. "Executed?"

"Crucified," I said.

"But He is not dead."

"He is," I said, "There's nothing left of what He was. Except on the island, after you showed me the men and women in the pit, there was a moment when He appeared almost as if—as if He was about to become Himself again."

"When exactly did this happen?" Gallus asked.

"As we fled toward the boat. Yeshua stopped me. He

looked back at the trees."

Gallus sat with this information. Then he said, "Pontifex told me once that, when looking at any mystery, there is always some element that does not belong. Beneath that element lies the truth. As a worm hides beneath a stone. And it would seem to me that your Yeshua is just such an artifact here in the Gray Palace, John. He has chosen to come to this place. He moves through the house as if searching. Perhaps whatever took place on the island came closest to what He is searching for. But at the same time—"

"At the same time what?"

Gallus shook his head. "Your friend is, perhaps, the key. But *how* He is the key, I do not know. I wish that Pontifex were here. He would tell us. He always understood better than I."

I gestured toward the door of our stone prison. "If Jax doesn't let us out of this room, I suppose it might not matter."

"You should rest for a time," the soldier said. "I will keep watch."

"Are you sure?"

"I am."

I nodded and went to Yeshua, taking His hand. I wanted to kiss Him on His bearded cheek, but I felt too mindful of the soldier's presence. Instead, I lay down at Yeshua's feet and, more quickly than I'd imagined possible, I fell asleep.

†

It was Thomas, great teller of tales, who once explained to me that dreams are the only place where the truth can be spoken. Everything else is lies. I tried to argue with him, but he persisted, saying that man cannot help but lie in words and acts and even prayers. "That is the nature of man," Thomas said. And there on the floor of the prison-like room, I dreamed. In my dream, I saw a great wooden door with a stone frame and hasps of hammered copper. I stood before the door, remembering what Thomas had told me. Soon, the door opened its eyes. For it had a thousand dark and roving eyes. The eyes of the great door found me and looked upon me. And when they did, I was no longer one man. I was, instead, multiplied. There were as many variations of me as the door had eyes. And I was suddenly everywhere, and all at once. Scattered in space and in time. A thousand Johns. A thousand histories. And the eyes read my histories as if my body was made of words. And, as they read, the words seemed to shift and change. And I too was changed, no version of me ever gaining permanence. I struggled against the eyes, fighting what they would do. Yet in the end, they triumphed. For when the eyes of the great door blinked, I disappeared.

†

I AWOKE WITH a startled breath on the floor of the cold stone room. The light of the torch had dimmed. Gallus lay on his back along the far wall, snoring, his bronzed armor gleaming in the light. I raised my head, expecting to see Yeshua still standing absently in a dark corner of the prison-like room. But Yeshua was not there. I sat up, heart quickening. Yeshua was not in the room with us. Gallus and I were alone.

I called out Yeshua's name.

There was no movement, no shuffle of feet.

I called out again, louder this time.

Gallus's rhythmic breathing stuttered. He opened his gray eyes. "John?" he said. "What is the matter?"

I stood, and the room seemed to tilt beneath my feet like the deck of a ship at sea. "He's gone."

The soldier peered into the dim-lit corners of the chamber, as if he might be able to see Yeshua where I could not. "That cannot be," he said. "I was asleep for only a short while. I would have heard if—"

"Jax," I said. "He must have returned."

"I do not sleep heavily," Gallus said, still sounding groggy. "I would have heard the door open."

The torch on the wall guttered and spat, threatening to go out.

Gallus directed his attention to the wall opposite the locked door.

I turned too and a saw something curious there. Running along the base of the far wall was a thin line of light, similar to the light that shines from beneath a closed door.

Gallus stood and approached the wall, lowering himself to his hands and knees. He attempted to peer beneath the wall. And when that proved impossible, he retrieved his sword from his belt and slid the blade carefully into the crack. The blade slipped easily under the wall, all the way to the hilt. "There is space beyond," Gallus said. "We could not see the light before because of the brightness of this room's torch."

"How do we reach the other side?" I said.

Gallus stood from his crouch and knocked against the stone, listening to the sound of his knuckles. "This may very well be a false wall." He attempted to slide the wall aside as if it was a door, but the stone would not move. Gallus turned his sword, gripping it by the blade rather than the hilt. "When we soldiers are trained," he said, "we learn that it is often more effective not to use the sword's blade, but rather to use the heavy pommel grip as a hammer and to strike a blow upon our opponent's head. I do not think I have ever needed a hammer more than at this moment."

With that, Gallus struck the hilt of his sword against the wall, once and then again, until pieces of stone began to chip away. Small pieces of the wall fell first, followed by larger pieces. "The wall is not thick," he said. "And the stone is brittle too." After striking the same spot with some twenty more blows, Gallus had opened a small hole. Yellow light streamed through.

Gallus put his eye to the opening. "By the gods," he said.

"What is it?" I hoped it was not another horror like the one we'd discovered on the island.

He backed away from the hole, an expression of amazement on his face.

I put my eye to the hole, and what I glimpsed beyond the wall actually filled my heart with joy. For I looked out upon a street in Rome. Not just any street, but the street in front of the Gray Palace. The meat market was there in the distance with the great pillared aqueducts beyond. Rome was full of so much color, hues I'd believed I would never see again: red terra cotta and gold-green tiles, statues painted crisp yellow and bright cerulean, standing proudly on the peaks of temples. In the distance, the Capitoline hill hovered like a frozen waterfall, a petrified cascade of great mansions.

We'd finally found the way out of the Gray Palace. And it seemed entirely possible to me that Yeshua himself might have somehow already escaped. We would discover Him waiting for us on the street beyond the wall.

"Stand back," Gallus said, gripping his sword once more by the blade. "There is a great deal more hammering to do."

As he worked to break through the wall, I walked the perimeter of the room and considered further explanations for how Yeshua might have escaped. Jax may have opened the door to the empty room while we slept, yet this seemed increasingly unlikely. The stone room had no windows. So, there would have been no way for Jax to verify that Gallus and I were both asleep. If Jax had opened the door, and we were awake, we could have rushed him and escaped.

Jax certainly would have wanted to avoid such an outcome. There was also the simple fact that Jax had shown no particular interest in Yeshua up to this point. What reason would he have for luring Him out of the room?

It was also possible that Sapia had opened the door. If she'd taken Yeshua and put Him in the hole in the wine cellar earlier, she might have come for Him in the stone room as well. Yet what motivation would she have for doing either act? And, like Jax, she could not have known we were asleep and, therefore, could not have known when she might safely open the door.

More likely than Jax or Sapia abducting Yeshua was the idea that He had wandered out of the prison-like room Himself. This had happened once before in the sacred woods upon our arrival in Rome. And then again when He'd wandered into the wine cellar and fallen into the pit. Therefore, the question had to be, if Yeshua kept moving away from me, what was He moving toward? What was His ultimate goal? Also, who or what force facilitated these movements?

I considered all of this while Gallus continued to widen the hole in the wall, allowing golden sunlight to stream through. And it was as I looked at that sunlight that I had a sudden and terrible realization. "Gallus," I said.

He paused, covered in sweat from his exertions. "What is it?"

"What hour was it when you entered the house?"

"Near evening," Gallus said.

"And what hour would you say it is right now according

to the light that comes through that hole?"

The soldier looked toward the hole but said nothing.

"More importantly, why is there is no sound coming from the street?" I said. "And no smell of animals from the market beyond?"

Gallus peered through the hole. "A dead world."

"Yes," I said, "yet another."

He lifted his sword by the blade.

"It's not a way out," I said.

"No," Gallus replied. "But it is at least a way forward."

†

WHEN THE HOLE in the wall was large enough, Gallus sheathed his sword and squeezed through the jagged opening. He called for me to follow. We emerged from the perimeter wall that surrounded the Gray Palace and stood together on the cobbled street before the house. It quickly became apparent that the notion of this being a dead world had been correct. The afternoon sky above us was a painted screen, as was the market square beyond. The cobbled street seemed actually more akin to a narrow hall. This realization brought about a feeling not unlike nausea.

"The door," Gallus said, pointing further along the gray wall.

I looked toward the replica of the front door of the Gray Palace that Sapia had invited me through earlier, and I saw the door stood open.

"The house is inviting us inside," I said.

Gallus nodded. "So it would appear."

†

WE APPROACHED THE door on the silent Roman street. The further we moved into the illusion, the more this house and street seemed slightly different than their counterparts in the outside world. Not only was everything lifeless and empty in this space, it was smaller too, fashioned to scale. As if the model in the map room had been enlarged, but not quite to full size.

I stood beside Gallus, and we peered together through the open door of the Gray Palace. This version of the entryway was identical in color and shape. But like the street and the wall, the entryway was almost imperceptibly smaller. And there was, of course, no Sapia to greet us this time. She was still with Jax in the other part of the house. Here, there was no one at all.

"Yeshua?" I called through the open front door.

The only response was a faint echo, accentuating the model house's haunted and forlorn aspect. It was as if life had moved on entirely from this place.

I looked down the exterior wall to the hole through which we'd recently passed. "Gallus," I said. "Do you think all of this is real?"

"What do you mean by 'real?'" he asked.

"This second house," I said. "The house inside the house."

"Why would it not be real?"

"We fell asleep," I said. "Perhaps we're now like the sleepers on the island. What if this is all some strange dream? What if our bodies are actually back in the doorless room growing gray moss?"

"Do not allow the house to steal your sense of truth," Gallus said.

"That's easier said than done," I replied. "We no longer even know if there is a Gray Lady. We might be searching for nothing inside someone's forgotten, endless maze."

"It is not endless. It is only a house."

"But what if you're wrong about that?" I said. "What if Pontifex was wrong?"

"We will see. And I doubt very much that Pontifex was wrong. Studying phenomena of this nature was his life's work."

"What if we disappear like so many others have?"

"We will not."

Another wave of affinity for the soldier washed over me. More than affinity, in truth. I felt something I did not want to name. "Gallus," I said.

"What is it?"

I looked into his gray eyes. "I apologize," I said.

"For what?"

"For not trusting you on the island. For telling you we didn't need your help."

"You do not need to apologize to me. Being a soldier is my duty. I perform that duty whether it is appreciated or not."

"Still," I said. "I'm sorry."

†

We passed together through the front door of the slightly smaller version of the Gray Palace, moving into the empty foyer. Memories of the original foyer overtook me. How simple the house had seemed when I'd first encountered it, how safe. I thought of Sapia with her kind greeting and reassuring smile, the flowers in her hair. Now, there was not even a whiff of such safety. There was, however, the black hall, leading deeper into the house. The hall that Sapia had explained was made of volcanic rock. This version of the hall was narrower than the original with a lower ceiling too. I had to duck my head as Gallus and I entered. I also had to will myself to resist reaching for the soldier's strong hand.

We made our way into the atrium, which was also slightly smaller in scale, but still impressive in its expanse. The skylight above the reflecting pool held within it another false and painted sky. Beyond the reflecting pool rose the fresco of the lotus-eaters. The sailors who'd fallen under some intoxicating spell lolled about, just as they had in the original fresco. I looked at these men as they dragged themselves through the field of otherworldly flowers, and I thought about how I too now dragged myself through such fields of illusion.

"Our sleeping quarters," I said. "Maybe Yeshua went there."

I made my way to the room at the back of the atrium, but found the space empty. There was a replica of our pallet there. And too, the low table with the flask of wine. I half-feared that I might find my leather satchel lying off in one corner of the room. But there was nothing like that. The room stood as it had when Yeshua and I first encountered it, clean and inviting.

Gallus and I left the sleeping quarters, and I led him back to the fresco of the lotus-eaters. I searched for the large white flower that Sapia pressed to open the door that led to the catacomb. I found what I thought was the correct flower and pushed several of its petals. But the petals did not move. No secret door opened.

"The atrium isn't the same," I said.

"Objects in dreams never are," Gallus said.

"You told me we're not dreaming."

"But this replica certainly makes me feel as though I am," Gallus replied. "I believe that is its intention. The dreaming state is important here. It is how the Lady makes her meaning. Perhaps it is also how she amasses power."

"So you believe there *is* a Lady even though Jax and Sapia have never seen her?"

"There is some guiding spirit," Gallus said. "And, I suppose, we can call that spirit the Gray Lady until we learn a better name."

I went to the door at the back of the atrium that had led to the false forest in the actual house. Above the proscenium was the same inscription written in a language I did not recognize. "Can you read it?"

Gallus peered up at the inscription. "An ancient

language," he said. "Pontifex schooled me in such things. He had a particular interest in the Etruscans, those men and women who lived in Rome before there was a city. This writing seems to bear some relationship to that study." He moved his lips, translating to himself. Then he said, "'Are we not all dead, entombed in the material dark?'"

"That's what it says?" I asked.

Gallus nodded.

"Uplifting," I said. And though I'd attempted levity, the words of the inscription troubled me. For so deep inside the house, they took on an even more potent meaning. I felt as though we were, in fact, entombed. There was no longer a Rome beyond the walls of this replica. Quite literally, there was only more of the Gray Palace surrounding us.

I wondered—did the dead dream? And if they dreamed, would their reveries produce an experience such as this? Did they walk forever in a silent house where rooms folded always back upon themselves?

As we passed through the door beneath the inscription, I wondered if we would encounter a false forest and an empty theater.

Would we be forced to experience everything in the house again?

But instead of discovering a forest, we were plunged somehow into complete darkness. I felt as if I had gone suddenly blind. I could not see my hands before me nor my feet below. "Gallus?" I called.

"I am here," he said from a place near my side.

"What is this? Why is it so dark?

"There are no torches, John."

"That's not what I mean."

"I know," Gallus said. "I was attempting to make a joke."

"Well, it wasn't a very good joke," I said. "What is this place?"

"We must continue on in order to find an answer to that question," Gallus said.

"But we don't know what's in this room," I said. "Or if it even is a room."

"Your Yeshua could be in here," Gallus replied.

The idea of Yeshua wandering in this darkness disturbed me. I did not want that for Him—fear heaped upon confusion.

"There is a perimeter wall," Gallus said from the darkness beside me. "I can feel it here with my hands. We should move separately around either side of the room."

"Separately?"

"We will be able to cover more ground that way, and we will find the next door. Time is of great importance, John. You told me yourself the Gray Lady will begin her celebration soon."

"But we'll be more vulnerable if we separate," I said.

"I have my sword," Gallus said. "And you have your knife."

"How do you know that I carry a knife?"

"I saw the outline of it quite clearly beneath your

tunic," Gallus replied.

I felt myself blush, and I was glad the room was dark so the soldier would not see.

"We will call to each other if we discover anything of significance," Gallus said.

"What if there are more gray sleepers here?" I imagined hundreds of moss-covered bodies lying dormant in the blackness. If I stumbled over one of them, the figure would open its eyes and clutch my ankle. The body would grin knowingly and make a hissing sound. And then the other sleepers would be roused, just as they were in the pit on the island.

"We will deal with the sleepers if it comes to that," Gallus said. "You will move along the right-hand wall and I along the left."

"I don't like this."

"Nor do I," the soldier replied. "Yet I believe it is the most efficient way to proceed."

†

WE SEPARATED THERE in the darkness. I placed my hand upon the cold stony wall as Gallus had instructed, and I moved along, shuffling my feet so as not to trip over something I could not see. Once, I'd entered a cave on the shores Galilee with Peter and Judas, and during our explorations there, our torch had gone out. Later, we all agreed that it was as if the world itself had disappeared. Snuffed out like some great candle. The black chamber in the Gray Palace made me feel as though there had never been a world to begin with. Everything that had once existed was only there to cover over this darkness, to protect the common man from knowing about the bleak infinity beneath. "Gallus?" I called, perhaps a bit too loudly.

"Yes, John?" His voice already sounded far away.

"Are you all right?"

"I am fine."

"That's good," I said. "I wanted to make sure."

"Keep your hand on the wall," Gallus called. "Move ahead. We will walk until we find a door."

†

As I walked, I pictured Yeshua's black eyes, flat and painted, as dark as the room where I now found myself. I'd sometimes felt so lost in those eyes, unsure what to say to Him, just as I felt lost now in this moment. I ran my hand up and down the cold wall, attempting to discern its height, searching for the door Gallus had predicted. The smoothness of the stone conjured images of his armor. I pictured myself touching the cold breastplate, exploring the hardness of it. I imagined sliding my hand up Gallus's warm neck, caressing his jaw. What would it feel like if the soldier kissed me? If I allowed him to touch me, even though he was a Roman. Even though he was part of that which had destroyed everything.

"Such a confused child," Peter whispered, suddenly beside me in the darkness.

I jumped, even though I understood the voice wasn't real. As always, it was a product of my own imaginings. And yet, there in the unnatural dark, the voice sounded more authentic than ever.

"You're the one who's confused." I whispered. "Just go away. I don't need your distraction now."

"But I want to watch," Peter said.

"Watch what?"

"Your undoing."

"What makes you think I'll be undone?"

"History." Then after a pause, he said, "Do you know what's wrong with you?"

"I'm sure you're going to tell me."

"You are potentially everything," Peter said. "But you're *actually* nothing. You've never made a choice in your entire life. You show no firmness of character. You have only the mad ramblings of your mother and your own diseased passions to guide you. I knew you'd fall under the sway of some other god sooner or later, John. In this case, a blonde soldier."

"I am not under his sway."

"At least Yeshua was special," Peter said, "worthy of your devotion."

"You don't know anything about Yeshua."

"Don't I?"

"You used Him," I said. "You wore him like a mask."

"And what did you use Him for, John? Did He want to

do all the things you did together in your private quarters?"

"Stop."

"Name the things you did with Him. How did you trap Him in your sickness? I've always wanted to know."

"You will be quiet, Peter!"

"Did you say something, John?" Gallus called from the far side of the darkened room.

"I was thinking out loud," I said. "I do that at times—to reassure myself."

"Understandable," Gallus replied.

†

THE FURTHER I moved away from the atrium door, the less I believed a second door would actually appear. I began to feel that this chamber where I found myself was not a chamber at all, but a vast empty space. Not empty in the same manner as the cell where Jax had imprisoned us. It was, instead, empty in a way that neither I nor any man had ever encountered before. I felt as though I moved away from time itself. The possibility of a "present" did not exist in the darkened room. I moved away from my own history too. From any sense of the past. I began to realize how easy it would be to become detached, to float away. My mother, in her current state, would not even recognize that I was gone. My father would think of me briefly, his pitiful, tormented son. And Peter would erase me from his story entirely. Who did that leave to remember me?

†

Some time later, I heard movement at my back, the scuff of a sandal, the rustle of rough cloth. I froze, listening. But the longer I listened, the more I believed there was no one behind me. Perhaps the room, the black chamber, had an echo. The sound was nothing more than the scrape of my own foot against the floor. I waited a few moments longer. And when I heard nothing still, I began to walk. But before I'd taken ten steps, another sound came. This time, a faint intake of breath.

"Peter?" I whispered, hoping it was nothing more than my imaginary companion.

But no one answered.

"Yeshua?" I said. "Is it you?"

Still, there was only silence in the dark.

I considered extending my hand, trying to feel for an invisible body. But what if it was one of the gray people from the island? Mouth open. Moss dangling from flesh.

I wanted to call out to Gallus, and yet I knew I'd feel like a fool if I asked him to come and rescue me from nothing. So instead, I decided to walk until I heard something more distinct.

I kept one hand on the wall as I moved. And though I heard no further sound, I felt as though a figure crept along behind me, sometimes closely and sometimes at a distance. But always, it followed.

"Who are you?" I said. "Speak up."

There was no response. I imagined a hand reaching for me in the darkness. Something that wanted to put its cold fingers around my neck.

"Gallus?" I called loudly. "Are you there?"

There was no answer this time.

I called again, thinking surely the soldier would respond.

But there was nothing. The void had devoured him. As it devoured all things. And I was alone with the invisible body that followed.

I remembered Peter's knife, black and cold like the darkness around me. I reached beneath my tunic and pulled the knife from of its makeshift sheath. I brandished the blade.

"Either come forward or leave me alone," I said.

But nothing came.

"I know you're there. I can hear you. This is your last chance. I have to find my friend. Do you understand? I can't allow you to hinder me."

I thought I heard another intake of breath.

I moved away from the wall in an attempt to force the thing to out itself. And when there was no further sound, I lunged forward with the black knife, making slashing motions. Yet my blade connected with nothing but air.

I began to believe the thing that followed me might be neither a man nor a woman, but somehow the darkness itself. Had the emptiness of this room become sentient? I crouched beside the wall, attempting to make myself as inconspicuous as possible. I didn't want the emptiness to see me any longer. I didn't want to give it the chance to touch me either. For to be touched by such a thing was to become it. I dropped the black knife and put my hands over my face. Soon, it seemed as if I grew smaller too, becoming the size of a child and then smaller still. A grain of sand. A mote of dust. I put hands over my mouth so as not to scream.

†

A POINT OF light appeared in the distance, shimmering there, bobbing up and down. I raised my head and watched as the light increased in size. How long had I been crouched on the floor? Hours or days? Or longer still? My first thought when I saw the light was that it was an indication of a doorway, a reason for hope. But the truth of the matter was that the light could not be a door because it moved toward me. I half expected to see some haggard spirit emerge from the darkness, a cruel specter come to devour me. But the light possessed no eldritch glow. And soon enough, I realized it was the beam of a lantern. When the lithe young man who carried the lantern came into view, I knew him immediately. Jax, still dressed in his gray tunic, moved through the black chamber, swinging the light from side to side. He no longer appeared serene as he had in the music room. In fact, he now seemed frantic. During one of the long swings of the lamp, he caught sight of me. And he was startled at first. Then he appeared to recognize me for who I was. "John?" he called.

Part of me worried he'd come to put me back in the

prison-like room. Perhaps he'd already captured Gallus and that was why the soldier hadn't answered my calls.

But instead of advancing, Jax called out again, voice trembling like a child, "Have you seen my sister?"

"What do you mean?" I said. "Where is Sapia?"

"I don't know," he said. "We left the conservatory. She was so upset. Terribly shaken by the thought that the Lady might not exist, that all our efforts were a folly. I hadn't seen her in such a state for a long while. Not since we were on Patmos, in fact. Not since our mother died. We returned together to the atrium. I tried to behave in a cheerful way. Just as I've always behaved with her. But Sapia wouldn't be calmed. No matter what I said. No matter how much I acted like Jax who'd been born feet first and always played a fool. I told her we must merely wait for the celebration. And she said, 'What if there is to be no celebration? What if there is to be nothing at all?' I told her not to think such thoughts. That she must, instead, busy herself. And she seemed to agree. She said she would get some bread and honey for us to eat in the atrium by the reflecting pool while we waited. Then she went off toward the kitchen."

"There's a kitchen?" I said.

Jax nodded. "Behind the weaver's room. But Sapia didn't return. She didn't bring the bread and honey."

"Well, where do you think she went?"

Jax shook his head. "I called for her. I searched. I fear that—I fear our Lady came for her."

"You told me the two of you were protected."

"I thought we were," Jax said. "But so much of what I believed doesn't mean anything now. You have to help me find her."

"You trapped us in a makeshift prison, Jax."

"That was for your own safety," he said. "You'd already awakened the sleepers on the island. I feared what might happened next if I allowed you to roam about."

I didn't want to help Jax find his sister. Very likely, she was merely off wandering somewhere in the house, as the two of them always seemed to wander. But I knew that Jax's lantern would certainly make my search for Yeshua and Gallus easier. And if I was with Jax, I would at least not feel quite so lost. "The soldier is somewhere in this room," I said. "We'll find him first. Then we'll find your sister."

"Sapia is close by too," Jax said. "She must be."

"How do you know?"

"Because there are only three rooms left in the house."

"Three?" The definite number surprised me. Nothing about the Gray Palace ever seemed definite. "Where did you get that information?"

"There's a map," he said.

"You're joking."

"I'm not. The weaver keeps it."

"How does the weaver have a map? Who drew it?"

Jax shook his head. "She was already here when we arrived from Patmos. She and her own twin, a man."

"The weaver has a twin?"

Jax stared off into the darkness, distracted.

"You're still keeping too many secrets," I said.

"I'm not. It's just—well—there isn't time to tell you everything."

"The weaver has a twin," I said. "Start there. Where is the twin?"

"We don't know. He wandered away one night. And they might not have even been twins. That was only a guess on my part. They might have been husband and wife."

"But he left the house?"

"We don't know that. How could we know?"

"Did you ask the weaver?"

"Sapia told me you met the weaver," Jax said. "Does she seem like the type of person who gives up information willingly?"

I thought of the silent woman who sat beside the loom. She seemed as dusty and disused as the rest of the house.

"We found bones once," Jax said. "Off the gray room with the turning wheel."

"Fortune's wheel."

"The bones were those of a man and a woman. Another pair of twins perhaps. Another pair of caretakers."

"How long has this been going on?" I asked. "How long have there been a man and a woman acting as caretakers for the house?"

"There's no written history. But if I had to guess—I'd say a very long time."

"How long approximately?" I said. "Tell me what you know, Jax."

"We should walk while I tell you," he said. "We must make our search."

"We'll walk," I said. "But you can't keep information from me. That's exactly the kind of behavior that will prevent us from finding your sister."

Jax appeared further sobered by this.

We walked then, and I called for Gallus while Jax called for Sapia. He held his lamp high, turning in slow circles. The thin, watery light of the lamp illuminated only a narrow perimeter around us. All the rest was darkness.

"Tell me about the final three rooms," I said.

"I know very little," Jax said.

"Don't lie."

"I've never been in this part of the house, John. We thought it was permanently sealed off."

"Who would do something like that?"

"I don't know."

"Well, what does the map say about the final three rooms?"

"It provides indications of their size and shape. The next room is large. The other two are much smaller. In fact, the final room isn't really a room at all. It's more of a hallway."

"And the hallway leads to an exit? You weren't lying about that, were you?"

"I've *never* lied to you about anything," Jax said.

"Are there doors?" I said. "Passages from one room to the next?"

"There are."

"What about the purpose of the house? What do you understand about its function? And don't say 'very little.'"

"I think of it as a machine," Jax said. "That's how I've always explained it to myself. There are gears and pulleys buried in the walls. I've seen them. They're connected to the siphons."

"Siphons?"

"Like those used in the Roman aqueducts," Jax said. "But there is no water for them to pull."

I thought of the drawings I'd seen on the desk in the sitting room and the small apertures I'd seen in the pit on the island. "What do the siphons pull in the Gray Palace if not water?"

"Air?" Jax said. "I don't know. I already told you. I'm looking at broken remains, just like you. I've simply had a longer time to study them."

Before I could ask another question, a stifled moan rose out of the nearby darkness.

"Gallus?" I called.

Again, the moaning. The voice didn't sound like the soldier's. It was weak, impossibly so. I hurried ahead, beckoning for Jax to bring the lantern. We found a shape slumped against the stony wall of the black chamber. It was indeed Gallus. He'd drawn his purple cape over his head like a hood.

I guided Jax's arm to bring the lamp closer.

Gallus looked up at us, squinting against the light.

"What is it?" I said. "What's happened?"

"I saw..." Gallus said.

I knelt beside him. "What did you see?"

"It passed over me..." Gallus said. "It passed over me in the dark."

"What was it?"

He rested his head against the wall. "Something terrible is going to happen in this house. We have to stop it. I have seen, John...we have to..."

†

IT IS HERE that I must pause and make what will likely prove a difficult point. The events that follow will be described, perhaps, not exactly as they occurred. Make no mistake: these *are* the events themselves. Yet, I cannot be sure that I've put them down correctly in words. For words, I have come to understand, are vessels. They each hold a spirit. And words are not the proper vessels for spirits such as these. Many of the things we encountered in the later part of our journey do not have names. Or, at least, they do not have names I know. And so, I have done my best to describe what I saw, to give shape to an outline. But there are certain emanations, certain states of being, that simply will not allow a line to be drawn. They find ways of freeing themselves, of creeping forth. Moreover, this confession applies only to the *first* of the three rooms. For there were, in fact, three rooms, just as Jax predicated. I have used words to describe what I saw and felt in the first of those rooms. And though they may not be the right words, I have, at least, managed to make images. The other two rooms were something different than that. But I've already said too much. Explanations prove impossible. I should only show you.

†

To BEGIN, I do not remember a door. I remember merely passing from the darkness into light. And after we passed from one state to the other, there was no longer the pretense of a house around us. Instead, we appeared to stand on a vast desert plain. A veil of white sky hung above. In the distance was a city, a vision such as I had never seen. It was not like Rome or Jerusalem or any place that could exist upon the earth. It was a kingdom of high bright towers and golden domes, of great bridges and pyramids and soring arches. It was the dream of a city. A fantasy, shining there upon the plain. And the closer we drew, the more I began to realize that the fantasy was also a ruin. For the gates of the high stony wall that surrounded the city stood open. There were no guards, only dust. And there was no music or noise of a market. There was only the sound of wind coming down off the high towers. A deathly, vibrating thrum.

"What is this place, Jax?" I said, looking at the dust as it churned in the open gate of the city. "You said there were three rooms. Is this some kind of trick?"

"I told you the room was large," Jax said.

"This is clearly *not* a room."

He rubbed the back of his neck. "There are many things we aren't meant to understand."

"And yet we must," I said.

"We will walk," Gallus said from behind us. He'd composed himself after his experience in the black chamber, regaining at least a semblance of his previous confidence. Yet he still would not tell me what he'd seen in the darkness. "We will pass through this city," he continued. "And there will be a door on the other side that will lead to further rooms."

"How could there be a door?" I asked. "What kind of door?"

Gallus didn't respond. Instead, he continued to trudge along through the sand. Jax and I followed him across the plain, drawing nearer the great golden ruin of the city with every step.

"Pontifex spoke of what he called 'capitals of the mind,'" Gallus said finally. "Hyperborea and Sodom, the Island of Atlas, the dark sprawl of Tartarus beneath the earth. He said such places normally exist only as we conjure them. Their bricks are made from the insubstantial thoughts of man. And yet I believe the Gray Lady has somehow forged just such a city here."

"How can you say she *forged* it?" I said. "She couldn't have built an entire city. And we can't still be inside her house either."

"The house has gotten bigger over time," Jax said.

"The sleepers make it grow."

"You must realize that makes no sense," I replied.

"I do," Jax said. "And yet—"

I thought of the city Yeshua had spoken of in His stories, the stories none of His disciples could properly remember. He spoke of a towered city, of temples made of gold. He'd lived there with His father. And He'd played with beings that could not be described as men. Was it possible this city was something like the place where He had lived?

"There are mirages in the desert," Gallus said.

"This no mirage," I said.

"Those who've see mirages would say the same," he replied. "Many men have died of thirst while walking toward a shimmering pool in the sand."

†

We soon passed through the broken gates of the city. The empty thoroughfares looked as if no one had walked upon them for a thousand years. Or stranger still, perhaps no man had ever lived in this place. For the structures were not built on a human scale. Instead, they were massive and monolithic, composed of hammered metal and great stone blocks that made my very soul feel insignificant. I studied the cold lines of a nearby tower and the smooth pinkish facade of one of the pyramids. The buildings that rose before us appeared to be neither shops nor temples nor mansions but great useless husks, rambling halls covered in arches and high peaked windows. I began to think of these structures as "temple-houses," though they had likely never served as either temple or house.

"Perhaps we should look inside one of these buildings," I said.

"We will walk ahead," Gallus replied. "Do not allow yourself to be distracted. The Gray Lady revels in distraction."

"But how do we know that Yeshua or Sapia isn't inside one of these buildings?"

"Because they are not," Gallus said.

"You sound very sure of yourself."

"I am."

"And why is that?"

"Because there is no city here. And if there is no city, there can be no houses. And if there are no houses, nothing can be inside of them."

"Gallus," I said.

The solider turned to look at me, jaw set, eyes hard.

"Tell me what you saw in the darkness of the black chamber. Whatever it was, it clearly haunts you still."

"Naming what I saw will not help us."

"It might," I said.

"We must press on."

I touched his arm. "Please."

He put his hand upon his sword and lowered his head. "I believe I saw what she intends."

"You saw it there in the dark?"

The soldier nodded grimly. "It passed over me."

"I'm not sure what that means," I said. "How could an intention pass over you?"

"I cannot say. What I saw was not rational."

"The two of you speak in irritating circles," Jax said.

"What would Pontifex tell us about the presence you encountered in the black chamber?" I asked.

"I do not know," Gallus said.

"Well, what did he expect to find inside the house?"

"He wanted only to speak with the Gray Lady," Gallus said. "To know her plans and the extent of her power."

I looked at Jax. "And you would not admit Pontifex for his investigation?"

"It's difficult to remember why," Jax said. "When someone knocks on the door, a feeling comes. Some men are permitted. Some are not."

"It was an arbitrary choice," Gallus said.

Jax shrugged. "I don't claim to know anymore, honestly."

"But you must understand something about these intuitions," I said. "What about your dream, Jax? The one you had on Patmos. The dream that brought you to the house."

"Everything I've told you about the dream is true."

"But you've given us no details."

"That's because I'm not permitted."

"Yet you said you would no longer conceal the truth from us," I said. "What if there's something in the dream that could help us find your sister?"

"There's nothing."

"What if you can't perceive it?" I said. "Because you've known the dream too long."

Jax closed his eyes and furrowed his brow. "I cannot tell the whole of the dream. But you can ask me questions, I suppose. I'll answer them if I'm able." He opened his eyes again. "But I'm only doing this because it might help Sapia."

I glanced at Gallus who nodded, indicating I should proceed. "Can you tell us the setting of the dream?" I asked. "Was it in this house?"

"A garden," Jax said. "It took place in a garden."

"And where was the garden located?" I thought of the paintings I'd seen in the house's sitting rooms. The Gray Lady stood in an alcove at the back of a Roman garden.

"I don't know where. I only saw trees and bright flowers."

"There was no wall?"

Jax shook his head.

"And what did you do in the garden?"

"I wandered," Jax said. "I thought it was all quite beautiful at first."

"At first?"

"That's right."

"And did you eventually stop thinking the garden was beautiful?"

"I did."

"And why was that?"

"Because I saw the birds," Jax said.

"Birds?"

"Large animals with great dark plumage and wrinkled faces. I call them birds, but I don't know if that's truly what they were. They clung to the branches of the trees. They had gleaming yellow eyes that watched over everything."

"What exactly was it about these birds that made you dislike the whole garden?"

"It was the way they looked over the expanse of it. The birds had been watching for a long time, forever perhaps. And they knew how false the garden was."

"Is this why you dressed as a bird in the theater, Jax?"

"What do you mean?"

"In the theater when I met you," I said. "You wore feathers and a beak."

"Oh," Jax said. "I don't know. I dressed like that because I believed the Lady wanted me to do so."

"And why would you think she wanted that?"

Jax shook his head. "I interpreted the signs. There was a feather in the atrium."

"A feather in the atrium meant you should dress as a bird?"

"You said you wanted to know about my dream," Jax said, squinting his eyes against the white light of the desert.

"All right. What does it mean that the birds believed the garden was false?"

"Such an idea would only make sense inside a dream," Jax said. "But I understood somehow that a garden was like a house. There was an architect. Someone who decided where the flowers grew. Someone who pruned the trees. And in my dream, I knew that a garden could never be *true*. It was made, constructed. The birds remembered what had existed before the garden. They knew the garden was a cage."

"The garden was cage?" I said.

Jax quoted from the inscription in the atrium: "Are we not all dead, entombed in the material dark?"

"What did the birds remember, Jax? What came before the garden?"

He shook his head. "Ask me something else."

"Can you not answer that question?" Gallus asked.

Jax rubbed his fingers through his stiff black hair. "I said ask me something else."

"All right," I said. "Did you see her in your dream? The Gray Lady?"

"Not in the garden," Jax said. "But gradually the garden changed. It grew into a kind of house. I saw the meat market beyond and the pillared forum with the statue of the minotaur. I knew my sister would be safe inside the house."

"And the Lady," I said. "When did you see her?"

"I saw her shadow," Jax said, "her gray shadow fell upon the house. It fell over everything."

Gallus held up a hand to pause our discussion.

"What is it?" I asked.

The soldier put a finger to his lips, indicating I should fall silent.

Then I heard a sound too, a shuffling movement and a

kind of ragged breath.

Gallus pointed toward the open door of one of the towers, gesturing for us to move inside. The three of us entered the tower, and Gallus led us quietly up a long spiral staircase.

"What is it?" I whispered on the stairs.

"Something approaches," Gallus said.

"But the city appears empty."

"It does." Gallus gripped the hilt of his sword. "And I do not think we want to meet the sort of thing that would choose to live in a place like this."

We left the stairs, entering a circular room at the top of the tower, high above the street.

Jax went immediately to the arched window and looked down. He gripped the window ledge and made a frightened sound.

"What's wrong, Jax?" I said.

"I should not have told you my dream," he said.

"You told us because it might help us find your sister."

"Our Lady won't forgive me now," he said. "I shouldn't have told you. Her secrets are meant to be kept."

I went to stand beside Jax at the window and, looking down, saw a creature trundling slowly along the street below. From the high tower, it was difficult to see the creature in any great detail. But I could tell that it was large and had a long worm-like body. Its skin was a waxy greenish color. The creature was naked, walking on four short legs. Or perhaps they should have been called arms and legs. For it appeared as though the creature could stand upright and walk like a man if it wanted to. The beast had an open mouth, a sort of hole that sucked air. Raw, bloody-looking vestiges hung from its back, appendages that might have once served as wings. The creature had a malevolent air, a poisonous aspect. And I knew it would bring great harm if it discovered us.

Gallus came to stand beside Jax and me at the window, and I found that I could not restrain myself in that moment. I reached out and took the soldier's callused hand.

He held my hand tightly in return and stared down at the creature.

The three of us watched as the long-bodied beast slunk slowly down the street.

I looked at Jax again and saw there were tears in his eyes. They dripped down his cheeks and fell upon the window ledge. He watched the worm crawl along the avenue until finally it disappeared around a corner. Jax took a breath. "If you see my sister," he said, "tell her our Lady knows what is best. Tell her I understand the mistakes I made." He paused. "No. Don't tell her that. Just say that I searched for her. I know that is the truth at least. Say I did my best to find her. But the house was too big. It has always been too big. Tell her that, John. Please."

And with that, Jax leaned forward, and before Gallus or I could grab him, he threw himself from the high window.

We watched as he fell down the length of the tower, gray tunic fluttering. His body landed with a terrible crack on the street below.

I leaned forward to look, and Gallus pulled me back. There was pain on his face. And something more than pain. Something that said he knew none of this made sense. It would not make sense. And there was no way out. But we could not do what Jax had done.

I fell upon Gallus, and he held me, grasping me tightly as a breeze came through the tower window to touch us both.

†

GALLUS AND I descended the tower in silence. We understood we would move forward through the city. Moving forward was all that remained. When we reached the tower base, I knew Jax would be there on the ground. I'd seen him from above, a crumpled mass. But I did not know the effect such a sight would have on me. Blood fanned out around his body like the rays of the sun. One of his legs was bent behind his torso. His arm was oddly raised, fingers splayed, as if he meant to summon us. His face had not been crushed. He lay there, mouth open, eyes half-lidded. I did not understand why he had leapt from the tower, other than the fact that there was nothing in this house but hopelessness. He believed he would never find his sister. We would never escape. All that could be done had already been done ages ago. Except for this. Except for death.

Gallus put his arm around me as we walked away from Jax and the tower. I did not, in that moment, fear the strange beast, the worm, that still stalked the streets of the city. I thought of its long body, its bloodied wings. I thought of the maddening face with the gaping mouth. The worm was the last thing that Jax had seen before his death. Perhaps the worm had somehow caused the death, as visions will, at times, cause a man to act.

Gallus and I walked down streets that bore a kind of glimmering sheen, as if they were made of something other than stone. I found myself wondering why the Gray Lady had put the city here. And I realized, almost immediately, that was an irrational thought. For how could a single person put a city anywhere? Yet I could not stop myself from thinking it. A house was like a garden. And a city was like a garden. All three had an architect. All three were false. But if the city around us was false, then what was the truth? Where did all these false avenues lead?

†

THE SOUND OF metal striking stone rang out in the street, echoing off the walls of the empty temple-houses. "What is that noise?" I said to Gallus.

He put a finger to his lips.

Together, we moved toward the sound. And in turning a corner, we encounter something strange indeed. A large hand made of stone lay on its side in the center of the street. The hand was so massive that it took up the entirety of the thoroughfare, like a hay wagon tipped on its side. I recognized the shape of the hand immediately. It was the same as the one I wore around my neck. The same as the door knocker that hung on the entrance to the Gray Palace. A woman's hand, long-fingered and open. As if the hand had once held something that was now lost.

A sculptor worked near the hand's wrist. He was an unkempt white-haired man, stooped and dressed in gray rags. The old man chipped rock from stone with a hammer and toothed chisel, evidently putting the finishing touches on his creation.

"Who is this?" I said softly.

"We are about to discover that," Gallus replied. Speaking louder then, he said, "Hail, good citizen."

The old man did not look up from his work. He strained as he hammered, ancient arms trembling.

"Sir," Gallus said. "We would speak with you."

I was not certain that we should speak to the sculptor. There was something troubling about the way he hunched over the hand, the way he worked so tirelessly, even though he was clearly exhausted. The whole scene unnerved me. But Gallus was not deterred. He moved toward the old man with a sure step.

"Sir?" he said.

And this time the old man ceased his work, not looking at us, but raising his head ever so slightly.

"Might we ask you some questions?" Gallus said.

The old man regarded us finally, first Gallus and then me, eyeing my gray tunic. "You have met her," he said, his voice a low rasp.

"Met who?" I asked.

"The weaver."

"I have."

The old man leaned his hammer and chisel against the sculpture. He lifted a leather vessel that contained water and drank from it.

"What work are you doing here, sir?" Gallus said, gazing up at the fingers of the giant hand.

The old man peered at him. "What work do I appear to be doing?"

"Sculpting."

"Then that is likely what I'm doing."

"I mean to ask—for what purpose are you sculpting?"

"It is what I do," the old man said. "Just as the woman weaves. We were once together. Now we are not."

"You cared for the house prior to Jax and Sapia's arrival?" I said.

"I do not recognize those names," the old man said.

"But you said you were the caretakers," I replied. "You and your—you and the woman. Was she your sister? Your wife?"

"She is neither," the old man said. "That was a long time ago. She is only the weaver now."

"But you came to the house together."

The old man squinted. "What house?"

I glanced at Gallus and saw that he'd raised an eyebrow at this.

"Are you not under the impression that you are

currently inside a house?" Gallus said.

The old man looked up and down the street. "Are *you* under the impression you are inside a house?"

"We are no longer sure," Gallus said.

The old man nodded.

"But you *were* in the house once," I said. "The Gray Palace. You acted as its caretaker along with the woman."

"Gray indeed," the old man replied. "There were vines that grew upon it. Valerian weed, as I remember. It was said that if a man ate of such a weed he would fall into the deepest of slumbers."

I thought of the sleepers, the moss that grew upon their faces. I knew something of Valerian weed, and I did not think eating it could have such an unnatural effect. Perhaps the old sculptor misremembered the weed, however. Perhaps the vines that once covered the walls of the Gray Palace had been of some other more extraordinary nature.

"How long ago did you come to the house?" I asked.

The old man picked up his hammer. "I need to work."

"Did someone give you instructions?" I said. "Did someone tell you to sculpt the empty hand?"

The old man considered my question. "We all attempt to please her in our own way, don't we?" he said finally. "That is how the house came to be. All of us searching for something that might please her. The weaver makes the tunics. And I make the hands. There have been others before us, a map maker and a painter, a writer of tragedies. So many others."

"Is this her hand?" Gallus said, surveying the sculpture. "The Gray Lady's?"

The old man nodded.

"And what was she holding?" I said. "It looks like something has fallen away."

The old man peered up at the long fingers. "Does it?"

"It does."

"Perhaps something has fallen away then," he said. "Perhaps she lost something dear to her."

"Have you met her?" Gallus asked.

"No one has met her as far as I know."

"But do you know where she is?" Gallus said.

The old man's expression shifted subtly, and I wondered if he was afraid. "You are searching for her?"

"We are," Gallus said.

"I would not do so."

"And why is that?" Gallus said.

"Why is that—" the old man repeated.

"It's a question I put to you," Gallus said. "Why should we not look for the Lady?"

"Because if you find her, what will you do?" the old man asked.

"We will speak to her," Gallus said. "Ask her questions about her intentions. About the meaning of this house."

"And what good would that do? Satisfy some curiosity of yours?"

"We have reason to believe that what she is doing here is dangerous," Gallus said.

"Dangerous for whom?" the old man said.

"For all of us," Gallus said. "For Rome."

"What is Rome?" the old man asked.

Gallus glanced at me and then back at the sculptor. "Where do you come from that you have not heard of Rome?" he asked.

The old man wiped his brow. "I come from a good many years ago," he said.

"But where?" Gallus said.

"There were fewer places then," the old man said. "Now I need to finish my work."

"Is this hand meant for the celebration?" I asked.

"Celebration?" the old man said.

"There's to be a celebration. That's what we've heard."

"Ah," the sculptor said. "I suppose it is then."

"Thank you for talking to us," Gallus said.

The old man continued to chip at the hand's wrist as we walked down the street away from him.

†

"DID ANY OF that make sense to you?" I asked Gallus as we walked.

The soldier considered my question and said, "I am beginning to think that all of Pontifex's studies were for naught. The house may be far simpler than he imagined."

"Simpler how?"

"It lays its intentions bare at every turn," Gallus said. "It causes those who enter to pass through the layers of a dream. Not our own dreams, but the dreams of the Gray Lady."

"And what purpose does that serve?"

"The house has the opposite of a purpose," Gallus said. "It dismantles the very idea of purposes."

I looked at the empty street ahead of us and then at the blank white sky.

There was nothing in this city. Only the sculptor and the worm. But what were they exactly? I wondered if Yeshua too had passed along these empty streets. Had he wandered in this city for a time? Surely He had because there was only one way of moving forward. Yet, I did not feel His presence. I did not feel the presence of Yeshua at all.

†

GALLUS AND I made our way down a series of wide boulevards, encountering a succession of temple-houses and towers, each eerily similar to the next. There were no market squares or spaces for festivals. But then again, why would a city need such spaces if it was not built for men? The longer we walked, the more I thought about Yeshua and the stories He'd once told in the olive groves. The only element that any of us could remember from those stories was the city. The place where Yeshua had once lived with His father and kept company with the playmates that were not like men. I wondered again if this city where I now found myself could somehow be *His* city. Perhaps He'd come to the Gray Palace intending to return home, to be with His father once more.

"Did Pontifex say that he believed the house might contain an environment such as this?" I said.

The soldier hesitated, then said, "He studied certain aspects of geometry. He was troubled by the house's angles. But he had no true idea of its content."

"I don't suppose anyone could have guessed such a thing," I said.

†

I AM NOT sure when exactly I realized there was no end to the city, that the shimmering streets went on forever, one nearly identical to the next. But I believe I know precisely when Gallus understood this fact. For he stopped walking and expelled an exhausted breath. He stood utterly still, as if he'd finally been transformed into the marble sculpture he so closely resembled.

"What is it?" I said.

He raised his head, gazing at the sky. The light had transitioned from white to rose and then finally to crimson. There were no clouds, yet there were no stars either. No hint of a moon.

"Night is falling," the soldier said.

"We should keep walking," I replied. "I'm sure we'll find the other door soon."

He removed his sword belt and went to sit on the lip of an empty fountain. "I am beginning to believe that is not the case."

"What do you mean?" I said. "We saw the city from its outskirts. We know, at least, that there is a wall, a perimeter."

"It *had* a wall. I am not convinced it does any longer."

"You think the city does not end?"

"I think it does not end for us," he said. "For others, perhaps. But not for us."

I sat on the edge of the fountain beside him. "Now do you think we are dreaming? I know I asked you before, but—"

"No," Gallus said. "We are not dreaming."

"Then, do you think we might be dead?"

He glanced at me. "Why would you say that?"

"Because how could this happen in the world we both know?"

"We are not dead, John. And we are not dreaming. But I agree we are also not in the world that we know."

I looked down the street, back the way we'd come. "How can the Lady have a world that is not our world, Gallus? Who would be powerful enough to do that?"

"That is the question, is it not? That has always been the question. But as I told you—night is falling. We should make camp."

"Where?" I asked.

"Inside one of these structures. We do not want to be outside, lest the beast from the tower return."

I thought of the creature we'd encounter, the scaly

worm with bloodied wings, and I shuddered. "Which structure?"

"Unfortunately, I do not believe it matters," Gallus said.

†

We made our way into one of the temple-houses and discovered a series of high-ceilinged stone rooms with no furnishings and no indication of purpose. The air smelled, not of dust, but of whatever might come after dust: the final decay of time. Though such a phrase was too poetic for the temple-house. Its rooms were brutally simple. We entered several more houses afterward and found that all of them contained bare spaces of a similar shape and size. Finally, we decided to take shelter for the night in one of the houses near an empty fountain, but not before we came across a small oil lamp on a street corner. Perhaps the lamp had once belonged to the sculptor or someone else who'd passed this way. Though I wondered what might have caused the traveler to leave so valuable an item behind.

As the vast cold room dimmed around us, Gallus lit the lamp using two pieces of flint from his pack. He then produced a crust of bread, broke it, and handed one of the pieces to me. I thanked him, yet it was not until I took the first bite that I realized how thankful I was. How long had it been since I'd eaten? My mouth watered as I chewed kernels of dried spelt. I had to wipe my lips so as not to drool on my tunic. Gallus, for his part, chewed the crust of bread in silence, seemingly unmoved. Whatever had passed over him in the black chamber appeared to hold him in its sway once more. He was slower in his gestures and pale, as if some vital energy had been sapped from him. This troubled me, as I did not want to find myself with another silent companion.

"Do you imagine our lamp is the only light in the whole city?" I asked, hoping to start a conversation, however meaningless.

"Unless the sculptor carries one as well," Gallus replied.

"You think he lives in the city?"

"I cannot say where such a man might live, John."

"And what about the creature, the worm?" I asked. "Do you think it might see our light and come to find us?"

"The house is fortified. The worm will not be able to gain entrance."

"That's one good thing at least," I said

Then we fell into silence. And as I finished eating the crust of bread, I attempted to imagine some kind of ritual that might have once taken place in the temple-house. I found myself picturing a funeral for Jax. Pyres burned and men in dark robes lifted their hands in prayer.

"Gallus," I said when I could remain silent no longer, "are you feeling better than you were before?"

"No," he replied. "I am not."

"Is it because of what you saw in the darkness?"

"It is."

"You told me you saw the Lady's intention there," I

said. "But will you now tell me exactly what you saw?"

"It will do no good."

"I felt something there in the darkness too."

Gallus looked at me. "Why did you not tell me this before?"

"You were troubled. Distracting you further didn't seem like the right thing to do."

"What was it that you felt?" Gallus asked.

"A presence. Something that crept along behind me. I think it nearly touched me once. A cold thing. It made me feel hopeless. Alone."

"I am sorry," Gallus said. "I would have come to your aid."

"Didn't you hear me call?"

He shook his head.

"If I'd known you were in trouble," I said, "I would have come to your aid as well."

His gray eyes softened, turning almost lavender in the lamplight. "It is rare that anyone comes to my aid."

"Well, I'm glad that you're with me," I said.

"And I am glad to be with you, John."

Without thinking, I reached out and took the soldier's hand, squeezing it with perhaps too much force. And just as a strong wind changes the currents of the sea, the act altered something between us. Gallus put his arms around me. The smell of him was all sweat and bronze. He kissed me. His mouth tasted sweet and dark like winter fruit. He pulled at my tunic, taking the garment up over my head and then removing the cloth from between my legs. I was naked in his arms. And he was so large. I realized I had not felt protected in far too long. I reached down to feel the stiffness beneath the pleats of his tunic. I wanted nothing more than to be with him in that moment. To forget the city. Forget the Gray Palace and the Lady. I even wanted to forget Yeshua. For if I thought of Him, wandering alone in the dark streets of the empty city, I would not be able to do this thing that I wanted to do so very badly. So I willed myself to forget. And there in the flickering lamplight, Gallus fell upon me, pressing me to the stone floor. He was no longer like some sculpture. He was all limber movement, glistening and bright. And when he was inside me, it was unlike anything I had ever known. I was no longer like myself. No longer bound inside my own skin. I dug fingers into his strong back, feeling his thrusts. I moaned for him, thanking him. And soon he was so deep that it seemed as though there was no city and there was no house. I was no longer forced to be John the Apostle or John the Beloved. And by the time the solider spilled himself inside of me, it was as if we rolled together beneath the dark waves of a body that was not the sea.

†

THE OIL LAMP still guttering beside us when I awoke later in the night. I remembered that Gallus had held me for a time, stroking my hair. Then he moved to the other side of the bedroll that he'd taken from his pack. I wondered briefly if his shifting had awakened me. But it was then that I heard a sound, a kind of wheezing breath, coming through the open window of the temple-house. I sat up and looked at the black window. Something was out there in the darkness. Something that watched us. "Are you awake?" I whispered to Gallus.

The soldier did not stir. I touched his shoulder and then shook him. But he merely brushed me away with one large hand.

I stood from the mat and picked up the oil lamp. The wheezing sound coming from the window made me think of the sleepers we'd awakened on the island. I worried that they'd followed us. And if there proved to be more than one of them outside, if there was a whole army of grinning mossy faces, I did not know what I would do.

I took the oil lamp to the window and gazed into the darkness of the city street. No one stood outside. Perhaps the interloper had moved on. Certainly, someone had been there only a moment before. Standing and watching. Gazing in at us.

I pulled Peter's stone knife from the makeshift sheath at my thigh and put my hand on the door. I worried that, if I opened it, gray figures would come spilling in. Yet the breath had sounded solitary. And if Gallus would not awake, it was left to me to make sure the temple-house remained a safehold.

I unbarred the door, wondering if I might actually find

Yeshua Himself outside. The thought of those empty black eyes looking back at me caused a pain deep in my chest. For though He would not see me, I knew He would cause me to see myself. Slowly, I pushed the door open. There was no one at the threshold. Nothing waiting to attack. I stepped out onto the cobbles, checking first to the left and then to the right.

Far down along the side of the building, a shadow stood, a male figure. He leaned against the wall of the temple-house, head lowered as if he was ill. It was not the old sculptor. And it was not Yeshua. The shape was larger in size than either of those two men, broader.

"Who's there?" I said.

The figure looked up.

I could almost make out his face, but not quite. To get a better view, I took two steps toward him. Then I saw. It was Gallus's partner, Magnus. The one who'd recognized Yeshua. He leered at me, appearing drunk.

"Magnus," I said.

The soldier took a single step forward, and I saw that the area around his mouth was covered in gray moss. He'd become infected. Though how this had happened, I did not know. There was blood on his temple too. And his face was bruised and swollen as though he'd been attacked.

"Jerusalem..." Magnus said, voice thin and cracking.

I felt frozen by the soldier's drunken stare.

"In...Jerusalem..." he said. Magnus sounded like a dreamer, repeating words in his sleep.

"Yes," I replied. "I was in Jerusalem."

He took another shuffling step toward me.

"Stop," I said. "I don't want to hurt you. Gallus wouldn't want me to hurt you."

Magnus's lips parted, showing gray mossy teeth. He pointed to the blood on his face, the bruises.

"Someone hurt you already," I said.

"Gallus..." he replied.

"Gallus is inside," I said. "I'll get him for you. We can all talk about this together."

Magnus shook his head slowly and pointed at the wounds on his face again. He made a fist. "Gallus," he said.

"Do you mean to say that Gallus did that to you?" I said.

He nodded.

"Gallus wouldn't hurt anyone."

Here, the soldier made the odd grinning expression. The expression was the same as the one that many of the gray people on the island made. A knowing look. As if they understood the essence of the world better because they'd been sleeping. They knew more because they'd dreamed.

"Gallus," the soldier said. "In the dark..."

"What?"

"In the *dark*..." he replied.

I realized suddenly what the soldier was trying to tell me.

"You met Gallus in the darkened room, the black chamber?" I said.

"In the dark..." Magnus repeated, gesturing to his face.

"And he did that to you there in the dark?"

Magnus grinned once more.

"But why would he hurt you?" I said.

"In Jerusalem..." he said.

"I'll wake him. There's been some misunderstanding. He'll make sure you are cared for."

The soldier moved quickly toward the door. He didn't want me to go back inside. That much was clear. And I certainly didn't want to draw too close to him. I didn't want to breathe the spores of the gray moss and become whatever it was that he was in the process of becoming.

"Gallus..." he said again.

"All right," I said. "Speak plainly if you're able. Tell me what you mean to say."

"Gallus...in Jerusalem..." he said.

"Gallus," I said. I looked toward the window and the darkness of our room where the soldier still lay sleeping on the bedroll.

"In Jerusalem..." Magnus said.

I wanted to call out, and yet any sort of action, anything too abrupt, might cause Magnus to lunge at me. I would maintain the space between us. I would not draw too near.

"You're making no sense, Magnus. If you could speak more plainly—"

The soldier coughed, wheezing. Finally, he said, "Did you...lay with him?"

I felt angered by this question, just as I'd once felt angered when Peter questioned me about Yeshua. "You saw us," I said. "You already know the answer. And Gallus told me you were in Jerusalem. He told me you recognized my companion."

Magnus leered at me. "*I* was..." he said. "And Gallus..."

"Gallus?" I said.

"In Jerusalem."

"He was not," I said. "He would have told me. He would have—"

"Hill of bones..." Magnus said. "And Gallus there..."

I felt as if Magnus was tearing at me with his teeth. Tearing my throat so I could not breathe.

Gallus had told me he'd left Rome to protect the borders of the Empire. He told me he'd gone to the East.

I tried to remember the day of Yeshua's death. A memory I'd built so many walls against.

The sky was no color. On the hill, crosses tilted like the masts of dark ships. There were crowds of men and women too. Those who had come to watch.

And then there were the soldiers. The bright circle of men.

I pushed through the crowd.

Peter and all the rest of the disciples had gone away. Even Mary had gone. They did not want to be captured by the Romans. They did not want to be imprisoned. Our war was over.

I stood alone before the hill of bones.

The soldiers stood in their armor of hammered iron and bronze. Eagles painted black and gold.

I saw Yeshua's face. His eyes rolled back.

I did not call out to the soldiers. There was nothing I could say to stop these men. They pierced Him with lances and spears.

Yeshua writhed.

Had there been a tall man in that circle? A Great Prince of the North? Had there been a hint of blonde hair beneath one of those helmets?

A man who would one day hold me in the dark.

Who would give me comfort in a city far away.

Outside the temple-house, I took a step back from Magnus. The gray moss had polluted him. Filled him with lies. My own mind spun like fortune's wheel.

Gallus.

I looked toward the window. The dark eye of it stared back at me.

In Jerusalem.

Gallus lay inside the temple-house. And I was in two places at once—in the abandoned city that could not exist and at Golgotha beneath the hill. I gazed up at Yeshua on the cross. I saw the soldiers. Vile men. How I hated them. And then I saw one soldier in particular, a tall figure with clean broad shoulders. He glanced at me only briefly. But I recognized the gray eyes, the set of his jaw. He met my gaze. "Gallus," I said. And something dissolved inside me, some belief, melting like wax.

I backed away from Magnus and the temple-house.

"Jerusalem..." Magnus said once more.

I ran, holding the oil lamp as tightly as I could, fleeing into the darkness.

†

I HURRIED DOWN black streets, the lamp extended before me. I stumbled on pavers, scraping my shoulders against walls. I believed, at first, that I would run until I found the exit. Until I escaped the blighted city and left its horrors behind. And yet I found no door. Of course I found no door. There was only one dark avenue after the next, all announcing the madness of the city, beating its rhythm on a drum. I thought of the soldiers at Golgotha. Men in armor. Men with spears. They too beat a rhythm. A circle of men around the cross. All the same. Faces the same. And yet not the same. For I could still feel Gallus inside me. Piercing me. Just as Yeshua had once pierced me. Not only my body. But some part of me that remained unnamable. And I had called out their names in passion. And they had held me. They pressed themselves to me. And my mother rose before me, face moon-white and damp with sweat, infinite, repeating: *In the beginning, there was emptiness and there was darkness...and when the heavens above did not exist...and when darkness was upon the face of the deep...and when the egg was finally cracked...when the egg was finally cracked...* She spoke in a rhythm, an incantation. As if the patterns of her madness might cause some new order to be born. And it was as I thought of this constant repeating, these stories from my youth, that I was stopped. For before me, curled in the brick lined avenue, filling the whole of the street with its girth, was the great winged beast, the worm.

I had made a grave mistake. I should not have run. I should not have been so reckless, so lost in my own thoughts. For now the worm would leap at me. Tear me with its teeth.

And yet, the creature did not stir. It slept, drawing slow and rhythmic breaths.

I lowered my lamp, hiding the light. But I did not run. Perhaps it was because I felt so broken. Perhaps it was because I was dissolved.

I studied the beast's serpentine body, some ten cubits in length. There were arms and legs. The arms ended in small nub-like fingers and the legs in vestigial toes. The appendages were short and thick, as though the creature was meant to drag itself on its belly. And the body was scaled, though some scales were missing, as the beast had an aged and weathered hide. Its head was neither the head of a serpent nor that of a man but something in between. The eyes were lidless. And so, like a snake, the beast slept with eyes open. The wings that it bore on its back were slippery and wounded. The creature made me think, once more, of Yeshua's stories. Stories of the great city where He'd lived with His father. Some of His playmates in that city, I remembered suddenly, had been winged. I'd always pictured birds. Surely, He could not have meant a thing such as this worm. This creature was monstrous in nature and would be the playmate of no one. Yet it struck me again that Yeshua had described some impossible city. And here I stood in an impossible city, gazing at a beast with wings.

Tales of exotic creatures were common enough. My mother, in her sleepless nights, had described the animals named by the Greek traveler Herodotus: the dog-headed men and the giant golden ants, the one-eyed cyclops and the feathered griffins, yet this worm did not seem like a creature from some foreign land. It seemed instead the sort of impossible beast that could not exist. Could not have ever existed. And I wondered if the Gray Lady had created the worm too.

I fell to my knees.

At that sound, the creature stirred, twitching one of its rudimentary arms and then a leg. I thought of Yeshua and of Gallus. I thought of what I had done in the temple-house. *In the beginning, there was emptiness and there was darkness.*

The worm lifted its human-like head. Its mirror dark eyes reflected the light of my oil lamp. The worm opened its mouth. Its maw was full of human teeth, and it made a sound like a dog and a bird. Like both animals screaming at once. And the creature scrambled to right itself. To come for me.

I no longer knelt. I ran as fast as I could.

The worm followed, half-clawing, half-flying. Flapping bloodied wings.

I could not gage how close at my heels the creature might be. But I did not want to turn and look. I ran down streets, fearful of pausing. For I knew that, if I wavered, I would feel the beast's fingers on my shoulders. I would feel its awful mouth. And it was as I imagined my own destruction that I glimpsed the open door of one of the temple-houses.

I ran for the door with the worm still following, still screaming, filling the city with echoes.

I dove into the open temple-house and slammed the door, barring it with the large piece of wood that leaned against the frame.

The creature smashed its body against the door once and then again, causing the very foundation of the temple-house to shake. Thankfully, the door held fast. I went to the single window on the first floor and shuttered it, glad that the stone of this building, like the stone of all the buildings in the city, was dense and strong.

The worm bellowed and then fell silent. And I found that its silence disturbed me more than its bellowing because I could no longer discern the creature's location.

I turned from the window and used my lamp to examine the room before me. It was similar if not identical to the temple-house where Gallus and I had made camp. The thought of Gallus caused my heart to twist. I attempted to push thoughts of him aside as I walked the perimeter of the large stone room, looking for some weapon that might serve me better than Peter's knife. A spear would be ideal. Something to slice through the belly of the worm.

From the first room, I entered a second and a third,

all of approximately the same size and shape. No murals graced the walls. No rug or furniture broke the monotony of the gray stone floors.

I walked into a fourth room and found there a spiral staircase. The stairs led to a second floor that was large and open. And though there was a narrow window, I did not bother to look out because the city remained dark. The only light was the light of my lamp, shining out into the blackness.

I realized, a moment too late, that my light would surely summon the beast.

And suddenly, the worm was outside the window, madly flapping its broken wings to hold itself aloft. It loosed its animal scream.

I stumbled back.

The creature reached an arm through the window, grasping with small thick fingers.

I backed my way to the far wall and leaned against the cold bricks, watching. There was no way for the creature to get inside. Its body was too big. Yet I found that I was frightened. For I knew I would never be able to leave this city. This was my maze. The worm, my monster. Yeshua was gone. Everyone was gone. I would be here forever and alone.

†

I AWOKE SOME hours later to the sound of knocking on the door below. I raised myself, still half-inside a dream. I imagined the worm knocking with its terrible fingers.

I rubbed sleep from my eyes. Light streamed in from the window. The sky had turned the bright color of morning, though it remained entirely without feature. No clouds. No sun. Nothing but an eerie glow.

The knock repeated, more insistent this time.

I went down the stairs, passing through the four rooms. Then, I stood staring at the door, imagining once more who might be waiting outside. It was certainly not the worm. Perhaps it was Yeshua. He'd found me here, just as He found me once before in the upper room.

The knock came again.

I went to the door and removed the bar.

Gallus stood at the threshold, sword in hand, looking as though he'd had no sleep. I backed away as if he was, in fact, the worm.

"John," he said. "It took me all night to find you. I followed the screams of the creature."

The hill of bones rose before me. Guards surrounded the base of the cross. Gallus and Magnus stood amongst them. Was that why Yeshua had approached the two soldiers on the streets of Rome? Because He'd recognized them? Because He knew what they had done?

"The beast is gone," Gallus said. "He has taken himself to some other street. You do not have worry." He stepped inside the temple-house.

"Back," I said.

"What?"

"Go back outside. Don't come near me."

Gallus appeared confused. "Is this because of what happened between us? I thought—I thought that was what you wanted. The same as I wanted—"

I pulled Peter's knife from its makeshift scabbard.

"What is going on?" Gallus said.

"Magnus came to the place where we slept."

"Magnus?" Gallus said. "How—"

"He's afflicted. The gray moss is on him. But he could still speak. He said he encountered you in the black chamber. That's what you hid from me. You didn't discover the Gray Lady's intentions at all. You only didn't want me to know that he'd found you. You fought him, trying to keep him away. Trying to keep him silent."

There was a part of me that hoped Gallus would act as though he didn't know what I was talking about. I wanted him to tell me Magnus had been lying. But the soldier only stood there in the empty room, staring at me in grave silence.

"Magnus told me you were both in Jerusalem. That you were at—"

"John," Gallus said.

"You knew," I said. "You knew all along who He was. And you tricked me."

"I *did* know," Gallus said. "I recognized Him the moment I saw Him here in Rome. I'd never born witness to a crucifixion before. You must understand. I remembered His face, long and narrow, full of pain. The horror of what was happening to Him. How could I not remember?"

"So you lied," I said. "All along. But for what reason?"

"I understood His coming held some meaning," Gallus said. "Pontifex told me there would be signs."

"You took Him as a *sign?*" I said.

"If a dead man walked up to you in the street," Gallus said, "would you not also take that as a sign?"

"I would not spin lies," I said.

"You told us He was your brother. You told us His name was Peter and that He was mute."

I wanted to say that such lies were not the same as Gallus's. Yet I found I could not open my mouth.

"When I saw the dead man, your Yeshua, I knew immediately that His presence had something to do with the Gray Palace. There is the witch's claim that dead men have been seen walking in and out its doors and night. And I wanted to discover whether or not He would go to the house. Whether He would be given admittance. I wanted to see if He might act as a kind of key."

"You used us," I said. "I thought you were trying to help. You told us to walk straight ahead. To walk directly into this trap."

"You would have gone to the Gray Palace whether I advised you to find a hiding place or not, John. You yourself said that it was He who took you here."

"So we were merely a means to an end?"

"I wanted desperately to complete the investigation that Pontifex had started with his father," Gallus said. "I wanted to understand. If not for myself, then for him, for his memory."

"And do you understand?" I asked. "Did any of this help you?"

"I gained access. I am here. I am still in the process of understanding."

"Is that why you lay with me too?"

"John—"

"Go," I said.

"Please."

"You destroyed Him once in Jerusalem," I said. "And you destroyed Him here again."

"I didn't want to hurt anyone."

"Yeshua—" I said.

"We can find Him together." Gallus reached for me.

"Together?"

"That's right," Gallus said. "What would be wrong in that? We want the same thing, don't we?"

"No," I said. "No, we do not."

"You will, at least, let me protect you," Gallus said. "This house is—"

"You have never protected me," I said. "Stand back. Stand away from the door."

Gallus hesitated, but finally backed away.

"You will not follow me," I said. "And I will not follow you."

He stood on the street, sword lowered. He looked like a child wearing a costume for play. We all wore costumes. Jax with his feathers and Sapia with her flowers. All of us played out some drama here in the house. Playing it at the behest of the Gray Lady. This was her ritual. We enacted it. Sacrificing ourselves. Preparing the way for whatever was to come.

I walked down the empty street, checking over my shoulder from time to time to make sure the soldier still stood where I'd left him. I hoped he would remain there forever.

†

THE CROWN OF thorns, a cruel circle. Bright drops of blood, stung from flesh. Nails for the hands. Nails for the feet. And how many wounds from Roman spears? How many calls for mercy? He could not control the muscles of His face. The convulsions of His eye and jaw. He bit into His lips, His tongue. By the end, He sounded like a braying animal. I felt His blood upon me still as I looked at the sky above the abandoned city. The sky was so pale. A shroud that covered the towers and the domes, as a shroud covers a body, as it is meant to conceal decay. And the beast, the worm, was out there somewhere in the maze of city streets. White maggot. Tunneling into flesh. I pressed my fingers against my eyes, causing flashes of light to streak across my vision. I strained to concentrate. I would not think of Gallus. I would not think of Calvary. Yeshua was out there somewhere. Yeshua needed my protection. I had to remain standing upright inside the tilting madness of this dream. I could not allow the house to topple me. It was not a puzzle.

Its rooms were not problems to be solved. But the city *was* a problem. It presented something that had to be worked out in order to make progress. In order to find Yeshua and to finally leave the Gray Palace behind.

I stood in the empty avenue, considering options, attempting logic.

I could try to return to the original gate that we'd passed through when we entered the city. Yet going back would mean very little. Retracing my steps would only lead me further back into the house. And I wasn't entirely sure that I could even find the gate. The city had no landmarks. It was, instead, an endless repetition. Temple-house and tower and empty fountain basin. There was, of course, the large sculpture of the hand, but where again was that?

I could try to find the old man, the sculptor. He understood something of the history of the house. I could attempt to glean more information from him. But I had a sense that this line of inquiry would quickly prove itself to be a dead end. The sculptor's knowledge had already revealed itself to be antiquated. He'd played his roll. And now, like his wife or his sister, the weaver, he was a kind of phantom. A ghost of the Gray Palace, enacting the same dream, day after day.

I considered the fact that I'd been attempting to leave the city by perpetually moving forward. However, it was not true that progress was always made in the Gray Palace by moving in a straight line. There was an "above" of the house and a "below" to consider. The catacomb where Yeshua had been trapped was below, as was the pit on the island. There were also the spaces above: the lift that travelled into the stars, the map room, the music conservatory.

Yet, when I gazed up at the white sky, I could not imagine any way to travel above the plain of the empty city. And likewise, I'd seen no entrances to any subterranean chambers.

I clenched my hands, pressing my fingernails into the soft meat of my palms, trying to think.

If I could not find a way to get above the city or below, and I could not find a way through the city, then what were my other options?

"There are none," Peter said from somewhere behind me. "You should understand that by now."

"There are always options," I muttered.

"Not if you're dead," Peter replied.

"I am not *dead*."

"Your body isn't. You proved that well enough when you lay with the soldier. But death is a varied thing, isn't it, John? There's physical death, of course. But there's also the death of the spirit. And what if this city is nothing more than a showing of your soul? It is empty because of what you and Yeshua forged together."

"The city is not my soul," I said. "And what Yeshua and I made together was good."

"Think what you will. It doesn't actually matter."

"And why is that?"

"Because, as you said yourself, you will never leave

this place. You will continue on, a wondering idiot, for the rest of your meager life."

I turned. Peter stood in the distance, a vague shape dressed in the brown robe of his youth, a length of fisherman's rope still tied about his waist. "And what about you, Peter?" I asked. "What will you do with your own life?"

"My life will be full," Peter said. "One of the fullest in all of history, in fact. And my works will be a lamp that shines for all eternity."

"At the expense of the men and women who would listen to you," I said. "At the expense of what is true."

"Do you claim now to know what's true?"

"Yes," I replied. "I know that truth is the opposite of—"

Then, in the shaded opening of the street ahead, I saw a long and slithering form. Broken scales. The sickly movement of wounded wings. It was the worm.

I hurried toward one of the temple-houses and pressed my body against its wall.

Thankfully, the creature hadn't spotted me. Yet, knowing the beast was so close, knowing that I could turn a corner at any moment and encounter its gaping toothy mouth was almost unbearable. If I wanted to escape this city, I could not allow the worm to corner me inside another temple-house, another empty room. There was no food and no water in this city. I would wither and die. I had to think, and think quickly.

"Thinking has never really been a strength of yours,

John," Peter called. "Nor taking action for that matter. A man is defined insofar as he acts John. But you are the disciple, are you not? You do not act. You follow."

Gallus said that the city was not a city. And it was true that nothing in the Gray Palace was ever what it pretended to be. So if the city was not a city, that might mean there was, in fact, no need to find a door. There were no doors. Just as there were no houses. If the city was not a city, I should be able to leave it at any point. I looked at the temple-houses around me. If the city was not a city, then what was it? It had to be *something*, for I stood inside it.

"So many stories in the olive trees," Peter said. "And you heard every single one. Yet, still, you did nothing. You sat and enjoyed the Manna."

I considered Yeshua's stories. Maybe this city was a story too, something half-remembered, like the city of His childhood. But no. I wouldn't be able to stand inside a story. I supposed some part of me could stand inside a dream, but the city was not a dream either. I was all too alert here, too filled up with pain.

"And dead," Peter repeated.

I wondered, for a moment, if he was right—was this a city of the dead? Not the death of the body, but the death of spirit? Could death become a city, just as life manifested in so many varied forms?

These considerations made me think once more of the worm. The creature was the only thing that seemed to have purpose in this empty place. The worm stalked and chased and hunted. The infinite array of streets were its home. Was it possible the worm understood the city better than any of us?

I ran my hand over the wall of a temple-house and thought: *Worm and maggot and king of the earth. The worm understands the dead city. And death understands the worm.*

†

ON THE NIGHT before the Romans took Him, Yeshua rested with us in the garden at the foot of the hill of olives. He sat upon a rock there in Gethsemane, as if the rock was His throne and the garden, a great palace. Peter and the others slept some distance away. Judas was already gone, doing what Judas would do. I sat with Yeshua, holding His hand. "We should leave," I said to Him. "Jerusalem isn't safe."

Yeshua made no response. Instead, He appeared to listen to some sound in the far distance.

"We'll go together," I said. "Find a village where no one knows us. We'll make a life for ourselves."

"We will stay here, John," Yeshua said finally.

I was not accustomed to Him making so definitive a statement, and I found myself confused. "But why would we do that, Yeshua?" I said. "It's only a matter of time before the Romans come. Before they take you away. You know that as well as I do."

"When you say 'Roman,'" Yeshua said, "what is it that you mean?"

I shook my head and squeezed His hand. "Cruel men. Brutal. Men who carry swords and—"

"But Romans are men," Yeshua said. "And wherever you take me, there will be men."

"Not *these* sorts of men. Men who would imprison you or worse."

"I've told you so many stories," Yeshua said. "You know by now there is only one place where I belong."

"The city beyond the desert," I said. "The city with your father."

"That's right. And I cannot return to the city beyond the desert."

"Yeshua," I said, kneeling before Him, pressing my cheek against His palm. "You have to listen to me. I care for you. I love you. I want nothing more than to make sure you are safe."

He studied me with His painted black eyes. "Do you like this garden, John?"

"What?"

"Do you like the song of the night birds? The scent of Calamus?"

I glanced around us, imagining that the tangle of olive trees was a circle of Roman guards. "It's not the garden I'm concerned with right now, Yeshua."

"Do you think Peter likes this garden?" Yeshua asked.

"No," I said. "Peter cares nothing for gardens."

"And you? Do you like this garden?"

I looked at the dark flowers growing amongst the

bramble. The vines and hidden ivies there. "No. I don't like it either."

"So neither you nor Peter like the garden."

"For different reasons, Yeshua," I said. "Peter doesn't like the garden because he cares only for his own power. And I don't like the garden because I know it is a place of danger."

"But I like the garden," Yeshua said. "And there were no gardens in the city where I lived with my father." He put His hand on my head and ran His fingers through my hair. "Why don't you kiss me now?"

"Kiss you?"

"You like the feeling of kissing me, don't you?" Yeshua said. "And I would like to be kissed here in the garden."

"You don't understand. There are so many things you don't understand."

"Our story—the story of Yeshua and John—was brief," He said. "The story that Peter tells will be much longer, I think."

"Our story could be longer too," I said.

Yeshua smiled. He tapped my chin lightly. "I'm not going to ask you again."

†

I CAUGHT SIGHT of the worm some distance away, moving at an odd loping pace down one of the empty streets of the city. The creature did not appear to be aware of my presence. It faced a direction opposite mine, grunting and snorting as it travelled. I pressed myself to a wall of another temple-house and watched. The worm hurried along, body undulating, bloodied pink wings shifting on its back. It moved with curious intent, as if preparing to take some action.

I slipped from the cover of the temple-house and followed.

Though I recognized this decision as a dangerous, I wanted to know what the creature understood about the city. Or rather, I wanted to know *if* the worm understood anything at all.

Something happened then that proves difficult to describe. For it seemed to me that a large hole appeared in the air before the worm. But "hole" is not exactly the right word. It might be more accurate to call the opening a kind of wound. A fissure in space that seeped and bled. The fissure did not appear to exist in precisely the same reality as the city. Instead, it lacerated the plain of the real. I thought, for some reason, of the black tunnel that led from the foyer of the Gray Palace to the atrium. That tunnel too had been a kind of dark and impossible wound, leading to a new realm.

I watched as the worm raced forward, quickening its loping pace. Then, with great suddenness, the beast leapt into the shimmering wound, flailing its arms and legs, scraping its wings against the rim of the hole as it wriggled to fit its great mass through.

Then, both wound and worm were gone. Vanished from the place on the street where they'd existed only moments before.

†

I MADE MY way toward the space where the worm and the hole had been. The air felt no different in that spot. There was no smell of sulfur, no shift in temperature. I turned in a slow circle, confounded. After a period of waiting, I walked on. For what else was there to do but walk? It was several hours more before I caught sight the worm again. This time the creature skulked near one of the empty fountains. The sky was vague and white above us. Temple-houses loomed over the street. And once more, I followed the beast. It crawled on its belly for a long while before beginning to move at the same curious loping pace as before. Soon, the shimmering wound appeared, bleeding darkly in the air. The fissure, I realized, was a kind of door. Perhaps, the only possible door. A tear in the very surface of the city. And I knew the only way to access what lay beyond would be to get close enough to the worm so that I could enter the wound directly behind the creature. Without thinking, I ran as fast as I could toward the worm, intent on passing through the wound just after the creature. But to my chagrin, as soon as the creature's head entered the hole, the entirety of its body was swallowed up. And so, instead of encountering a passageway myself, I encountered only air. Once again, the worm was gone and the shimmering fissure had sealed itself.

†

I WALKED THROUGH the city for several hours more, worrying I would not find the worm again. Perhaps the beast had decided to remain in whatever place it found itself after passing through the shimmering fissure. But such concerns proved unfounded, for I located the creature soon enough. It lay coiled and sleeping at the base of one of the odd pinkish pyramids that appeared in the city with far less regularity than the temple-houses or empty fountains beds. I waited some distance away, contemplating the sleeping worm, watching the way that it sometimes fluttered its freshly bloodied wings. Perhaps the worm dreamed of flight through the empty skies above the dead city, a flight that it could never achieve in life. I looked too at the creature's all too human face. It was something like the face of an adult male, though greenish in color like the rest of its body. Even in sleep, the face had the expression of despair that falls permanently over some men as they grow old. The worm's open mirror-like eyes stared at nothing.

I waited for an hour more, and finally the worm uncoiled itself and began to trundle along on its short malformed legs. I followed for a time before the worm began the odd loping run that I knew indicated the wound was about to open in the air. I raced after the worm and just as it pushed its face through the shimmering fissure, I summoned every ounce of my courage and jumped onto the creature's back, grabbing handfuls of its bloodied wings. The worm let out an angry scream, somewhere between the cry of a man and the howl of a wild dog. And then, quite suddenly, we were both passing through the wound that had opened at the center of the street.

†

WIDE LEAVES AND dark blossoms. The unfurling of tremendous flowers. The world became suddenly dense and lush. And the worm was gone from beneath me, perhaps dissolved or slithered off into the mad and verdant foliage. I found myself in what I perceived to be a garden, overgrown, nearly primeval. My first thought was that it must be another of the Gray Palace's artificial environments, not unlike the forest or the lake. Yet, the more I studied the plant-life, the more I realized I couldn't be sure if the flora was false or true. I touched a large leaf and found that it seemed to be made of silk. But when I tore the leaf from its stalk and rubbed it between my fingers, a grassy scent arose. The blossoms of the flowers were much the same. The petals appeared false at first, as if made of dyed papyrus. And yet there was a smell about them and a softness that indicated the natural world. The plants before me were somehow neither false *nor* true. They were something in between.

I heard singing in the distance then, a woman's voice. I stepped behind a tree and kept watch, remembering how Jax said he'd heard the Gray Lady singing behind the wall in the prison-like room. Perhaps it was the Lady herself who sang here in the garden. The song was lilting and bright, a paean to joy. Then I saw a figure dressed, not in a tunic, but in a loose-fitting garment made of gray feathers. She'd likely borrowed the costume from her brother. Sapia, auburn hair loose about her shoulders, a garland of wildflowers at her brow, walked amongst the plants, gazing at them with admiration. She moved with ease and delicacy. The distress she'd exhibited in the music room was gone. She was at peace here, at one with the garden. And even before I revealed myself, Sapia appeared to realize someone was near. She paused her song and said, "Who is it? Who's there?"

I stepped out from behind the tree. When Sapia saw me, a new light filled her. She shone amongst the leaves and flowers, a kind of human flame. "John," she said. "You found your way."

"I suppose I did," I replied, unable to stop myself from thinking of Jax's body crushed on the street beneath the tower. Sapia did not know her brother was dead. I felt sorry for her because of this and wondered if such news would douse the flame inside her.

"Our Lady will be so pleased you've come," she said.

I glanced around the garden. "Is she here?"

Sapia smiled. "No. Not here."

"But you've seen her?"

"She summoned me," Sapia said with great pride. "Just as she once summoned Jax on Patmos."

"And you've spoken with her?"

“Everything is clear,” Sapia said. “There’s no need to talk when all things have been made so clear.”

Jax believed he would never find his sister again in the vast house. And I wondered whether this was, in fact, Sapia standing before me. She seemed different in some fundamental way. A vast spirit disguised as a girl.

“What exactly has been made clear to you?” I asked.

Sapia laughed, though I wasn’t sure how anything I’d said could be interpreted as funny. “John, do you know why I admitted you and your friend to the house?”

“I don’t.”

“I believed I exercised my own free will,” Sapia said. “I thought, here are two men who look weary. They are clearly tired from the heat of the day. Wouldn’t it be good to let them rest? But now, I understand I was wrong about my motivations.”

“Wrong in what way?”

“When I admitted you, I felt our Lady’s will for the first time. I finally felt the true *meaning* of the house.”

“The meaning?” I said.

“I understood you were necessary,” Sapia said. “I knew the moment I saw you. I even thought that you and your friend might be our next caretakers. But I’ve realized now you are something more than that.” She stroked one of the leaves in the garden. “Our Lady knows who you are, John. She knows your friend too.”

I felt a rush of panic at this. “Where is Peter?” I said. “Have you seen Him?”

"His name isn't Peter," Sapia said calmly.

"No," I replied. There was no longer any reason to lie to her.

"Tell me what you call him."

"Yeshua," I said.

She looked amused once more. "And you know as well as I do that isn't his true name. He's like our Lady, isn't he? He doesn't have a name."

"Where is He?" I said.

"Very close," she said. "Everything is so very close."

"But has the celebration begun?"

"That's something we didn't fully understand either," Sapia replied. "Jax read the signs incorrectly. The celebration is a flowering of our Lady's efforts, that much is true. But it isn't something that will happen once. It's going to happen all the time."

"Has it begun, Sapia?"

"Come," she said. "There's something I have to show you. A task granted to me by the Lady." She turned and began to walk deeper into the garden.

†

I FOLLOWED SAPIA through the tangle of tall plants. There was no path, so we had to move carefully, pushing aside leaves and great nodding flowers. As we walked, I began to wonder about our precise location. I'd passed through the hole in the plain of the city, the bleeding wound in space. So did that mean we were still in the city? Were we within the walls of the Gray Palace? Or was I now somewhere else entirely?

"Sapia," I said. "Can you tell me more about the last room in the house?"

"The last room?"

"The room beyond this one."

"You mean *her* room, John," Sapia said. "Our Lady's own chamber. That's where you'll finally meet her."

"I don't want to be surprised," I said. "There have already been too many surprises in this house. Could you tell me more, please?"

Sapia looked at me with something like compassion. "I'll tell you what I know. But I cannot promise that what I say will make sense to you."

"I'll listen," I said. "I'll try to understand."

Sapia spoke, describing what she understood of the Lady. Her words felt like a further unfurling of petals and leaves. By the end, the garden around us seemed even denser than it had before. Sapia concluded by saying, "She fills me up now, John. I understand her will as she has always expressed it. As she has spoken it to so many men and women over the centuries."

"But what is that will exactly?"

"To reveal the fallen nature of things," Sapia replied.

"Fallen?"

"That's right. She's going to help us leave all of this behind." She touched my arm. "You'll see. I promise."

†

"Most of the house," Sapia said as we walked, "was built by men and women who were summoned by our Lady. Caretakers, just as Jax and I are caretakers. There have been so many ages of stewards here. So many who attempted to understand her will. Jax and I found the bones of some of the men and women who came before. But there were many others too. Caretakers whose bodies turned to dust long ago. They all felt our Lady's will. They heard it whispered in the halls. Some saw it written in the water and the trees. And they interpreted that will. They took action based on what they believed to be her wishes. They made the forest and the amphitheater, the island and the stars. All things they supposed would help the sleepers to dream. All things they believed the Lady wanted. But there is one piece of the house, one and only piece, that our Lady built with her own fine hands. I'm going to show it to you now."

"And why will you show me?"

"Because you are important, John."

I stopped. "Why would I, of all people, be important here?"

Sapia turned, looking oddly grave. "You don't want to know the answer to that."

"I do. Tell me."

"It will only trouble you, John."

"I don't think anything could trouble me after all I've been through," I said.

Sapia tilted her head. "All right. You are important here because of your current state of being." She caressed a leaf. "I'm going to sound something like a philosopher when I explain this, I'm afraid."

"What state is my current state of being?"

"It's difficult to describe, as all such states are. But I will try. Your current state of being is something similar to non-existence."

I stared at her, believing she would say something more, that she would qualify this statement somehow. When she did not, I said, "Non-existence? You think I don't exist? I thought you were mad when I met you, but now you are verifiably so."

"I told you that you wouldn't like my answer," she said.

"I expected something sane."

"I knew the moment I saw you that you were different. It wasn't that you and your friend looked tired. That was merely how my mind described it at the time. That was all I could comprehend. Now I realize that you seemed instead to hover just outside of being."

I lifted my hands, moving my fingers. "Do you see this?" I said.

"I do."

I tore a handful of leaves from one of the nearby plants. "And this?" I said, dropping the leaves at her feet.

"You needn't hurt the plants, John."

I put my hand on Sapia's shoulder and squeezed it. "What about this?" I said. "Do you feel this?"

"I feel your hand," she said. "You have a body, I agree. But you do not exist in the same way as other men. Neither you or your friend. You are both like the house."

"The house exists," I said.

"Does it?"

"I entered through the front door. I met you in the foyer, and I met Jax in the theater. I found Gallus on the island and then—"

"Yes?" Sapia said.

I thought of all that had happened, attempting to hold the events in my mind. "I was raised as a fisherman on the shores of Galilee," I said. "My companions and I met a stranger there. Only He wasn't a stranger to me. I followed Him. He said He would tell me things He could not tell the others, and— " I faltered, feeling anger well up inside me. "I don't have to explain my existence to you."

"No," she said. "You don't. Now, please come along, John."

†

WE PASSED DEEPER into the garden, and I had a sense of something moving in the far distance. I looked into the shadows there and saw what appeared to be the shapes of very large birds, plumed creatures shifting behind the trees. The birds were as big as oxen. Larger still in some cases. One seemed as big as my father's fishing boat and another was as large as the temple in Jerusalem. "What are those creatures?" I asked.

"I don't know," Sapia said.

"Birds?"

"Do they look like birds to you?" she asked. "I had some vague idea that they might be the first of the caretakers. But I think it's best not to pay much attention to them. They are beyond us. As many things are beyond us here. They don't have to explain their existence either, you know?"

†

WE CAME THEN, not to a room, but to a kind of walled grove within the garden. There was no door, only a feeble stone arch raised as an entrance. Sapia and I passed together into the space the Lady had built with her own hands, the very first room of the Gray Palace. This was the seed from which all else had grown. And there at the center of the walled grove, two pieces of wood had been nailed together. I thought, at first, that the Lady had built a cross like the one at Calvary. A central pole with a beam nailed to it. It leaned in the same way as those crosses on the hill of bones, as though it might collapse if a strong wind blew. But it was not a cross, not in the same manner as those I saw at Calvary. It was, instead, meant to be a tree. There were leaves carved into the surface, scraped into the wood by some stone implement, a primitive, ancient tool. And too, there were carvings of fruit. The tree bore a great deal of the fruit. Sapia and I walked together around the tree. Then we approached it, and she put her finger into the groove of one of the carved fruits. I reached up and did the same. Sapia smiled. "Thank you for helping my brother try to find me," she said. "That was very kind of you."

"Your brother," I said, "he—"

"You don't have to speak the words," she said. "I already know. Everything our Lady sees, I can see. My brother was confused for a long time. He misunderstood our Lady's signs. But he loved me. He cared so deeply for his sister. And I loved him as well." Sapia broke off. "It's time for me to leave you now. Time for you to meet her."

I found that I was afraid. And my fear felt like a wound opening.

"There is a door," Sapia said.

I saw it then, a rustic wooden door, behind the tree the Gray Lady had built.

I heard too a faint hissing in the distance.

"The sleepers are awake," Sapia said softly. "They are coming, and they know the meaning of their dreams. You must go now. Hurry, John. She wishes to see you alone."

"Will she give Yeshua back to me?" I said.

"Yes, she will give Yeshua back to you."

†

I WENT TO the rustic door and opened it, imagining, in that moment, that I might be excreted from some crack in the cosmic egg. I'd ooze forth like so much human yolk. Or maybe I'd be set aflame, as those men in the old stories are burned when they dared to look upon a god. But, in truth, very little happened when I opened the door. Beyond its threshold, I saw, not a room, but a long hallway, just as Jax had predicted. The hall was made of wooden planks, split pieces of an ancient tree. The edge of one plank had been laid upon the next to form a kind of tunnel made of wood. And I found I could not see the end of the tunnel, either because it was too long or too dim or perhaps because it was both. In the space before me were two chairs. They faced each other. One chair was empty. And in the other sat a tall female figure, bolt upright, unmoving. Her posture led me to believe she was frightened or somehow in pain. The figure in the half-dark reminded me of my own poor mother, sitting alone in her shadows, whispering: *There was a time when we were good, John. When the gods still came to visit us*. But when I entered the room, I realized the figure was not a woman at all. It was some kind of model or sculpture made to look like a woman, hands placed palms down upon its thighs. The sculpture was dressed in a gray garment that was not a tunic but something more primitive, a piece of fabric with a hole cut in the center for the head to slip through. The fabric seemed a mere gesture toward clothing, but not actually clothing itself. The statue's eyes were closed like that of a sleeper. Its skin, made of some earthy substance, was gray and had the dry cracked texture of a pot that had been fired too long in a kiln. The statue had rust-colored hair that was not actually hair but some kind of coarse dried weed, inserted into the scalp, stem by stem.

As I entered the room, I experienced an odd sensation. I felt as if the statue might somehow have become aware of my presence. Energy shifted, brushing across my skin, seeming to examine every part of my body.

The rustic door closed behind me then. And I was alone with the gray statue.

I looked toward the darkened part of the long wooden tunnel and wondered if there was another door hidden there, the exit Jax had promised. Jax said he had never lied to me, and if that was true, the door must be there. But in order to walk down the tunnel, I would have to pass by the statue. I reminded myself that the figure sitting before me was only a body made of clay. Yet as the floorboards creaked beneath my feet, my muscles tensed. I feared I would somehow be recognized. Though I did not know exactly what such recognition might mean.

I took three steps into the room, and as I walked, I pictured Sapia in the garden, moving amongst the plants and singing. I thought of Gallus too, in the city, standing alone in the empty street. I thought of Peter in Jerusalem, speaking to the crowds. I thought of Jax, dead beneath the tower.

I took three more steps.

Then the statue did what I'd known it must do the moment I saw it sitting in the chair. It opened its eyes to look at me. Only what was revealed beneath the gray lids were not like eyes. They were more like holes. As if some weary sculptor had hastily pressed his thumbs into the unfinished face long ago.

The statue did not speak. Instead, a subtle energy shifted in the room. An energy that was almost visible. I was acknowledged. Though I did not feel as if I was acknowledged as John. I was acknowledged merely as a substance. A substance had entered the space of the room. A substance that was recognized.

Near the ceiling of the wooden room were what appeared to be stone ports, the siphons Jax had mentioned. Whatever was harvested in the house—some product of the dreamers—was drawn into this room. It acted as the energy that surrounded me. It moved freely about the space.

The statue in the chair did something even more remarkable then. It lifted its stone hand very slowly. It turned the hand so the palm faced the ceiling of the room. The statue appeared to gesture toward the chair opposite its own.

I did not want to sit. I did not want to allow the statue to further observe me with its strange, hole-like eyes. But I realized I had no real choice. I was sealed inside the wooden room with this figure. And I had every sense that the statue itself had closed the door, using the energy that surrounded its clay body.

I went to the chair and sat before the figure.

The statue blinked, slowly and deliberately, as though it had learned long ago that blinking was an action all living people did. And, therefore, blinking was what the statue must do to behave as a person. There was something else about the blink too. The slowness of the gesture seemed to indicate weakness. The statue was not altogether well. The blink looked, in fact, like the winding down of an old machine.

The statue gazed at me with eyes that were not like eyes, seeming neither asleep nor awake, as if its consciousness existed in some middle realm. And I thought that I must seem both a man and a dream in whatever served as the statue's thoughts.

After a long silence, I spoke because I realized that I must. Time did not move in the same way for a statue. I was the one who had to act. The statue had been waiting in this room for a very long time. "Where is Yeshua?" I said.

My question hung in the air between us. The words, all too solid for this space.

The statue continued to stare at me.

"Who are you?" I said.

The statue turned its head with terrible slowness. I could hear grinding in its neck, the gears of broken machinery. Eventually, it regarded the closed rustic door through which I'd come

"Why did He come to this house?" I said. "Why did Yeshua come here to you?"

The statue continued to gaze at the rustic door that led back to the garden.

"Please, speak to me. Tell me where He is."

I thought I heard some sound beyond the door. The scrape of a hand. Then a hiss. The sleepers, I thought.

The sleepers, with their grinning moss-covered faces, had found the door.

The statue, the figure whom Pontifex had referred to as the Great I Am Not, turned its head slowly back to look at me once more. The expression on its stony face had changed ever so subtly, eyes opening wider, the corners of the mouth turning down. What precisely this new expression meant, I could not be sure.

Another sound came from behind the rustic door. One loud thump and then another. Something wanted in.

I looked into the statue's eyes and realized they were not eyes at all, but rather stony caves. They were like the cave where we had buried Yeshua. I saw Him standing in a dark corner of His burial cave, shroud draped over His head. He stood in the darkness before Peter and I arrived to push the stone away. I thought of Him rising alone from the bench where we'd laid Him. I thought of Him standing for the first time since His death on the cross. Moving His bones. Moving His flesh. What was the first thing He did after He stood? Had He walked to the stone that blocked the entrance to the tomb? Had He made the sounds that Mary Magdalene heard, the scratching upon the stone? Or had something else made those sounds? Something that wanted Him set free?

I studied the statue who sat before me, understanding some event was about to take place. The statue needed to draw energy into itself in order to perform an action. It needed to draw energy from the house, from the siphons.

The sleepers dreamed. Even though they were now awake, they continued to dream. And did they give the figure the energy it needed in order to perform its final acts? Or was it somehow Yeshua and me? Were we the necessary dream?

The statue rose from its chair. The action was a labor, a ruin of centuries. Its body rose as if from death, though I knew it had never lived. It stood before me. And I felt afraid. Because the statue was not like a human. But it had the semblance of a human.

The statue held out its hand to me. I looked at the hand and saw that the fingers were long and thin, the very same fingers as the knocker on the front door of the Gray Palace, the fingers of the totem I wore around my neck. Fingers that had once held something of great meaning. Something that had been lost.

I stared at the hand and finally took it.

The statue's fingers felt like the dry earth.

†

THE FIGURE GUIDED me down the creaking wooden tunnel, shifting the boards of the great dead tree as it moved. I could see nothing in the distance. Nothing but shadows. Soon it became clear that, in the dim-lit tunnel, there were etchings upon the wooden walls. The etchings showed a woman in a garden who stood beside a large tree covered in fruit. And there was a serpent in the garden too, long-bodied and winged, coiled about the trunk of the tree. I recognized the serpent as the worm from the city. The worm and the woman had lived together in the garden. The images on the wall were done in an unschooled hand, the scrawling of a child. I heard my mother murmuring her stories in the dark: *In the beginning, there was emptiness and there was darkness...and when the heavens above did not exist...and when darkness was upon the face of the deep...*

"You are the woman in the garden," I said, "But you are more than that too."

The statue did not reply.

When we walked again, it was as if we moved through water. The statue drew more energy into itself. And I was, once again, the man who followed. We moved through the dream of the sleepers. The statue hesitated only once more, stooping, unwell. Another sign of the machine winding down.

"What is it you intend?" I asked the statue.

I heard Sapia then, as she had spoken to me in the garden: *Our Lady has been given many names, John. She is called Sophia, meaning 'wisdom,' and Eva, meaning 'breath' and 'life.' She is called the 'Aeon Who Fell' and the 'Dream of the Dust.' And there are those who would know her as 'She Who Spoke to the Serpent' and 'She Who Ate from the Tree.' But you must understand that all these names were forged by men. Our Lady reminds us that she has no name. For names and stories and all the rest are part of the terrible and broken illusion. The illusion that is called God and Earth and the Cities of Man. Our Lady is one who existed before in the endless gray brink of the Pleroma. And she remembers what it felt like to float there in her quintessence with no name and no story. She knows the gray was good. The gray was good, John. Our Lady wants to deliver all of us back to that nameless place. Not just the caretakers or the sleepers, but everyone in all the world. And now, because you and your friend have come, she has finally found the key. She will fling the doors of her palace wide. And together we will celebrate the great undoing.*

Up ahead, I saw a body lying on the ground, a male figure in a gray tunic. The figure was crumpled like some forgotten doll.

"Who is that?" I said.

That statue made no response.

I let go of the long-fingered hand and went to the body. I knew who it was even before I reached the form. The bony shoulders, the lank dark hair. I called out Yeshua's name but He did not move. I went to Him and knelt beside Him, touching His shoulder, turning Him to face me. I realized that I looked at a corpse. Yeshua was dead. His dark eyes were open, clouded. I saw the old spear wounds in his side, milky with decay. The marks of nails in his hands and feet. His flesh was bloated and peeling. He smelled of rot and looked as if He had been dead for many weeks.

I turned to the Gray Lady, the heat of tears in my eyes.

She looked at me with eyes that were like caves and siphons and pits of endless depth.

"Why did He come here?" I asked. "Did He know

what you would do?"

The statue said nothing.

"Did you do this to Him? Did you take something from Him?"

She knows the gray was good, John.

And now that you and your friend have come, she has finally found the key.

I stood, trembling. I was not a key. And Yeshua was not a key. We were men who had loved each other. Men who had tried to find a way together. Couldn't I at least be sure of that? I threw open the door at the back of the house and saw it led to an alley in Rome. Morning had dawned. Sun glinted off the black soot of the filth-stained bricks. A magpie that had recently inspected some remnant of discarded meat fluttered its wings and flew away. I lifted Yeshua's corpse by the arms. The statue watched me, eyes like wounds that led to some other world. I pulled Yeshua into the alley and knelt there, holding Him. I looked back at the Lady in the shadows. And as I watched, she raised her long fingered hand and showed me that she now held something small and spherical in her palm. It was not a fruit from an ancient tree, but a starlit thing that contained the tatters of the false Earth and the layers of the illusory Heavens. Beyond all of that lay the gray expanse. The Pleroma, as Sapia had called it. And this was the map. The knowledge the Lady had lost so long ago. Yeshua had somehow returned it to her.

Behind the statue, down the long dark hall, the rustic door burst. The hissing sound intensified, a thousand frenzied serpents. The sleepers were coming. They knew the meaning of their dreams, the intentions of their Lady. And they had come to celebrate.

Then, the door to the Gray Palace closed. And I sat alone in the dirt, cradling the body of Yeshua in my arms. We had escaped. Yet it seemed to me there was no Rome and no Jerusalem. There was no Sea of Galilee. All of it was an illusion painted on a scrim. I wondered if Sapia was correct, and we too, Yeshua and John, Beloved and Lover, might merely be figures painted somewhere in the endless halls of an old ruined house.

But no, that could not be. We were more than that.

I closed my eyes and pressed my face against the rot of Him. In the darkness behind my eyelids, I heard the hollow echoes of my mother's voice. I heard Peter too, telling story after story in the olive groves, reminding us of all the things Yeshua had never said and never done.

I hugged Yeshua's body tightly, kissing Him gently on His mouth.

And then, I was in the desert where I'd wandered as a boy, following a snake, straying far from my village. This was the desert in which I'd searched for the limits of the world. But I was not alone this time. Yeshua was there with me. And He looked healthy and alive.

I stood before Him, astonished. "You were dead."

His painted eyes glinted darkly in the desert sun. "No, John," He said. And His voice sounded just as it had on the shores of Galilee.

"But I held your body in my arms."

He touched my cheek. His hand was warm. "It's possible you misunderstood."

"The statue," I said, "the Lady. Do you know her? Did you come to the house to meet her?"

"We knew each other long ago," Yeshua said. "She was a playmate and then a kind of mother to me."

"A mother?"

"You're not the only one with a mother, John." Yeshua said, half-smiling.

"Was it in the city that you knew her? The city where you lived with your father?"

"Beyond the city, as I recall. I could tell you the story. But I don't think you'd remember in the end."

"Yeshua," I said, "the woman in the house, Sapia, she told me I do not exist. That you do not exist."

"Don't we?" He held out His hand to me. "Come along. We should go."

I didn't move. I no longer wanted to follow anyone. Not even Him. Yet He waited there patiently. And finally, I said, "Where do you want to go?"

"First, I think we should find the solider," Yeshua replied. "We shouldn't leave him out here all alone. That would be unkind. And we are not unkind."

"But Gallus—the things he did."

"And after that, we'll find the young man who fell from the tower."

"Jax is dead."

Yeshua gazed off into the desert. “Don’t you see the past receding, John?”

“If I go with you,” I said, “will you tell me the whole story—about the Gray Lady and her house and where you came from before you met us by the sea—even if I can’t remember, will you tell me?”

“Yes, John,” He said. “I promise. I’ll tell you.”

I looked at the desert before us, the gray horizon there. And I wondered if this sky and this earth were finally true or if they were yet another mere illusion. Soon, I realized such questions didn’t matter. This was the world for now, as much as any other. I took Yeshua’s hand in mine, and I did not follow Him. Instead, we walked together, our shoulders nearly touching.

ACKNOWLEDGMENTS

My gratitude to Steve Berman for his support of this novel and for creating such an excellent and important home for the speculative and the queer at Lethe Press. Thank you also to my thoughtful and diligent agent, Eleanor Jackson, who has provided invaluable guidance over our years of working together. Thank you to my colleagues and students at Vermont College of Fine Arts and the University of California Los Angeles Extension Program, all of whom consistently help make the creative process feel engaging and new. Thank you to Brian Leung for championing my work and acting as an always compassionate first reader. For their help with this novel and for their friendship, I'd like to thank Christine Sneed, Scott Blindauer, Mike Shackleton and Gabriel Blackwell. For our frequent discussions about Los Angeles and all the Gray Palaces we've discovered there, thank you to my friend Chris Baugh. Thank you also to my mother; my father; my brother, Kory; and my sisters, Sarah and Elizabeth. Sarah read countless drafts of this novel as I worked on it, helping me every step of the way. And finally, thank you to Brad Beasley for his support and love. His kindness, sweet humor, and will toward adventure are a constant inspiration for me.

ABOUT THE AUTHOR

ADAM MCOMBER is the author of *The White Forest* (Touchstone) as well as two collections of short fiction *This New & Poisonous Air* and *My House Gathers Desires* (BOA Editions). His short fiction has appeared in *Conjunctions*, *Kenyon Review*, *Black Warrior Review*, *Diagram* and numerous other magazines and journals. He teaches in the MFA Writing Program at Vermont College of Fine Arts and in the Writing Program of the University of California Los Angeles Extension.

CPSIA information can be obtained
at www.ICGtesting.com
Printed in the USA
LVHW092328230321
682287LV00007B/328